HOLME FOR THE HOLIDAYS

MIRANDA MACLEOD

Apple Blossom Press
Bolton, MA

Holme for the Holidays

Copyright © 2016 Miranda MacLeod

All rights reserved. No part of this publication may be reproduced, distributed, or transmitted in any form or by any means, including photocopying, recording, or other electronic or mechanical methods, without the prior written permission of the publisher or author, except in the case of brief quotations embodied in critical reviews and certain other noncommercial uses permitted by copyright law.

Find out more: www.mirandamacleod.com
Contact the author: miranda@mirandamacleod.com

ISBN-13: 978-1547204793
ISBN-10: 1547204796

This is a work of fiction. Any resemblance of characters to actual persons, living or dead, is purely coincidental.

Apple Blossom Press
PO Box 547
Bolton MA 01740

ALSO BY MIRANDA MACLEOD

Telling Lies Online

Holly & Ivy (cowritten with T.B. Markinson)

Love's Encore Trilogy:

A Road Through Mountains

Your Name in Lights

Fifty Percent Illusion

Americans Abroad Series:

Waltzing on the Danube

Holme for the Holidays

Stockholm Syndrome

Letters to Cupid

London Holiday

Check mirandamacleod.com for more about these titles, and for other books coming soon!

ABOUT THE AUTHOR

Originally from southern California, Miranda now lives in New England and writes heartfelt romances and romantic comedies featuring witty and charmingly flawed women that you'll want to marry. Or just grab a coffee with, if that's more your thing. She spent way too many years in graduate school, worked in professional theater and film, and held temp jobs in just about every office building in downtown Boston.

To find out about her upcoming releases and take advantage of exclusive sales, be sure to sign up for her newsletter at her website: mirandamacleod.com.

HOLME FOR THE HOLIDAYS

ONE

"WHAT THE HELL am I supposed to do with the twenty-seven pound turkey in the kitchen sink?" As a pithy comeback to a breakup speech, Paige knew it fell short. She might have opted for 'How could you do this to me?' or 'I thought you loved me' if she'd had even a few seconds of warning to prepare a response. But Veronica's announcement had come out of the blue, and Paige's concern for the turkey, though lacking dramatic flair, was a valid one. That monstrous, plastic-wrapped beast took up so much space that she could barely fit a glass under the faucet. It still had three days left to thaw before being stuffed and roasted to perfection so that it could occupy the place of honor at the first Thanksgiving dinner that she and Veronica had planned to host in their own apartment. It was an event which suddenly seemed unlikely to occur, given Veronica's announcement that she would be settled somewhere across town by then.

Veronica blinked languidly, looking confused. "Why did you buy such a big turkey?" She leaned against the counter in their shared kitchen where Paige was peeling potatoes, her casual attitude in stark contrast to the fact that she'd just flipped their cozy domestic partnership on its head.

"What do you mean why? To feed our guests, that's why. Along with ten pounds of potatoes and enough pumpkin to make four pies. Between your family and mine, we're expecting at least twenty people for dinner on Thursday."

"I never actually said my family could come, if you'd been listening." A flash of something more potent than annoyance flitted behind Veronica's dark eyes, and Paige felt an icy stab in her gut. In the eight years they'd known each other, their relationship had never been perfect. They'd even broken up a few times before. But this was the first time when Veronica had said that things were over that the expression in her eyes backed up the claim. "In fact," she continued, "there's really no way they could. My grandmother's coming into town."

"Your grandmother?" Relief surged through her at the revelation, returning the warmth to Paige's extremities. "So that's what this is about."

The matriarch of Veronica's family was as traditional as they came, and she ruled her clan with an iron fist. If she was making a rare journey from Taipei to San Francisco, it was no wonder Veronica was behaving like she was. The last time the elderly woman had visited, she and Veronica weren't even dating yet. They'd been nothing more than roommates in school. Well, they *might've* fooled around once or twice, but it hadn't been anything serious. Even so, Veronica had insisted they stack their dorm furniture into bunk beds just so her grandmother didn't jump to any uncomfortable conclusions that might have led to her threatening to cut off Veronica's tuition payments. When it came to her grandmother, Veronica was famous for her extreme measures.

"You know how she is." Veronica's smile was soft, apologetic. Paige's heart melted into a puddle in her chest.

"It's just, when you said you were getting an apartment, I thought you were breaking up with me!" Paige chuckled at her own misunderstanding. "I didn't realize it was just for show. So, how long do you have to stay there to placate your family before you can move back home?"

Veronica studied her fingernails thoughtfully, her eyes downcast. "The thing is, I'm not sure that's something we need to rush."

Paige frowned. "I don't understand."

"Paige-y," she said with a laugh. Paige bristled at the nickname, which Veronica only used to butter her up. Experience told her that whatever she was going to suggest next, Paige wouldn't like it. "We're *so* young!"

"We're twenty-six. People our age get married and start families all the time!"

"Marriage? That's the furthest thing from my mind right now, and don't even start about kids. *This,*" one hand gestured with a sweeping motion that encompassed the surrounding apartment, "is already too much. I just don't think I'm ready for it all right now. I mean, to have a dining room table, for God's sake, and twenty people coming over for dinner?" She rolled her eyes as if to dismiss the ridiculousness of the notion.

"I wasn't suggesting marriage. Or children. And *you* were the one who bought the dining room table."

"I know. And it's going to be such a pain in the ass to get out of here, too. Thank goodness my parents are paying for a mover." She glanced at the hulking mass in the dining nook, forehead crinkling. "Do you think you're going to need that orange tablecloth you bought for it? It would be perfect on my mom's table on Thursday."

Paige stared at the festive table cloth she'd bought for the dinner they would no longer be hosting and blood-red spots formed at the edge of her vision. "I really don't care what happens to the fucking tablecloth, Veronica."

Veronica's eyes widened, wounded. "There's no reason to talk to me like that, Paige. It's so crass."

"Oh, I'm sorry." Her words oozed sarcasm. "How

am I supposed to talk to you while you're breaking my heart?"

"Breaking your...*Paige-y*. You're being melodramatic." She reached out and smoothed a stray lock of Paige's bright purple hair tenderly back into place behind her ear. "I know you. You say you're not talking about forever here, but it's what you're thinking. It's *always* what you're thinking. And it doesn't work for me right now. Hey, don't mope like that!" She brushed her finger along Paige's cheek, dragging it teasingly down her throat until it rested in the hollow between her breasts. "Just because I don't think we should live together doesn't mean we won't still see each other. I love you. You know that."

"You still want to see me." Her body was on fire from Veronica's touch. It would be so easy to give in, to agree to do it her way and accept the reward that Veronica's roaming hands promised. But desperate as she was for affection and validation, something didn't add up. Paige's eyes narrowed and she pulled away from Veronica's touch. "But you want to see other people, too, I assume."

"Well..." Veronica gave a half shrug, confirming the obvious.

Paige slammed the peeler in her hand onto the counter, sending a dozen slippery white potatoes cascading to the floor. She stormed out of the kitchen and toward the bedroom without another word. Her blood boiled. Her relationship with Veronica had always been complicated. On again, off again, all through college and beyond. She should have known it would come to this. But when Veronica had finally agreed to living together, she'd thought...*Never mind what I thought. I couldn't have been more wrong.* She shut the door and leaned her weight against it as the fight drained out of her, hot tears burning her cheeks. A tap on the door made the wood vibrate against her back.

"Paige?"

She lifted the chunky black glasses from the bridge of her nose and wiped her eyes, her still-messy fingers leaving a slimy trail of potato starch across her damp face. "What do you want?" *Please say to apologize. Please just say it was all a misunderstanding.* She knew she was pathetic for wanting that, but she couldn't help it. All she wanted was Veronica.

"Paige, my clothes are in there. I need to get in so I can pack."

Paige's breath rushed from her lungs as though her girlfriend's words had delivered a physical blow. That she was more appropriately called her ex-girlfriend now was too painful for Paige to contemplate. She tore open the door, barely taking in Veronica's stunned expression as she pushed past her into the living room, then marched straight to the front door and all the way to her parked car without stopping. Her hands fumbled with the car keys, her breath coming in gulps as she sank into the driver's seat and dug in her pocket for her phone.

"Call Brittany." Her voice cracked as she gave the command, too shaky to trust her fingers to navigate the screen. "Brit, I need a place to stay tonight," she said when her best friend answered. Asking was just a formality. Unlike Veronica, Brittany had never once let her down. With tears blurring her vision, Paige started on the drive through thick fog and Bay Area traffic toward Sacramento.

"SHE'S A SELFISH BITCH, Paige. She always has been." Brittany slid a steaming mug of coffee to within inches of the spot where Paige's head rested on the kitchen table. Her crisply pressed suit stood in sharp contrast to Paige's day-old ensemble, now rumpled beyond redemption from a night of fitful sleep in Brittany's guest room. "I know you've been in love with her since your first day of freshman year, but you must have figured out by now that this kind of crap is a major part of the whole Veronica package."

"That's not really fair," Paige's words were muffled by the cool Formica tabletop. Her hair formed a messy cloud around her head, like neon-purple cotton candy that glowed in a beam of early morning sunlight. "We've had our ups and downs, but most of the time it's been perfect. We can finish each other's sentences like we're the same person."

"But is that because you really want the same

things, or because you've convinced yourself that whatever Veronica wants must be what you want, too?"

"Of course not! This is mostly because of her grandmother, I think."

"Seriously?" Brittany sighed, then her voice took on an angry edge. "You switched your focus to classical music in school because Veronica didn't like jazz. You've spent the last six months playing extra gigs with three different chamber orchestras, which you hate, to afford your share of the rent on that overpriced, trendy apartment *she* insisted on. Now she moves out without a moment's notice and you're just letting her off the hook like that? You've gotta stop defending her, Paige."

"I'm not!" Paige lifted her head from the table and forced her body upright, reaching for her coffee and letting the steaming liquid coat her raw, tear-ravaged throat. "But families can be challenging. Plus, her grandmother pays for a lot of her bills."

"That revelation doesn't increase my sympathy for her, just so you know."

"Her family might support her financially, but she doesn't get the emotional support from them that she needs." No matter how broken she felt inside, Paige couldn't muster the same righteous indignation that her friend felt on her behalf. Loving Veronica was a hard habit to break.

"Oh, the poor little lambie-poo." Brittany punctuated her sentence with a derisive snort. "That makes it all okay, then."

Paige shot her friend a warning look. "Do you know how lucky I am to have a supportive family? Not everyone has that, that's all I'm saying."

Brittany arched one perfectly groomed eyebrow. "You know I love your family like they're my own, but it took your mom a year to be able to say 'my daughter' and 'her girlfriend' in the same sentence without bursting into tears. And I don't recall Veronica being very understanding about it at the time, either. Especially considering she was the one who outed you in the first place."

Paige wrinkled her nose at the observation, but couldn't completely deny its truth. As her best friend since elementary school, Brittany had been around to witness her whole coming-out process as it played out in real time, and it hadn't always been a smooth road with her family, or with Veronica. "Mom's much better now. Even if she does still question how things might have been different if we'd moved back to Minnesota when we had the chance."

"You would have gone to college to study handbells instead of piano. And you'd still like girls." Brittany's typical bluntness made Paige grin.

"It's good to know that even in an alternate reality, I'd still manage to disappoint Mom in all the ways that really matter." Despite their issues, though, Paige knew her mother was on her side when it mattered most. "Plus, if we had moved, she wouldn't have you, her almost daughter, to brag about. Do you know how many times I've heard about your practical college degree and solid government job?"

"*With* a pension." Clearly, Brittany was familiar with the speech.

"Oh my God, the pension! How could I forget that? And you're a homeowner, too." She laughed as Brittany gave her a playful slug to the shoulder, then sighed heavily as the full weight of her predicament hit her. "I need that audition with the Bay Area Symphony Orchestra to work out more than ever if I'm going to be able to keep paying the bills."

"Again with the classical music, Paige. That was what Veronica wanted, but it's never suited you. Remember when you used to talk about playing in jazz bars, or hell, doing movie scores?"

"Neither of which offer health benefits like the BASO does. They gave Veronica a great plan when she started with them." She groaned. That was just one more thing she'd have to deal with post-breakup. She'd been set to go on Veronica's plan as a domestic partner, but that wouldn't be happening now. "That audition's my best bet."

"You mean the one Veronica's setting up for you. Do you really think that's still going to happen?"

Paige frowned. "I don't see why not. I know you have a low opinion of her, but there's no reason to think she won't be able to separate her personal life from her professional one."

"Maybe not. But can you? Think about it, Paige. What would it do to you to see her there every day?" Brittany paused to let the words sink in while Paige fidgeted with her coffee mug. "What if she started dating someone else at work and you had to see them together all the time?"

"I..." Paige's shoulders slumped. "I don't know. But I don't have a choice. I've gotta pay rent."

"How about getting a roommate?"

Paige shook her head. "No good. It's a one-bedroom apartment. Even if it weren't, I can't imagine sharing it with someone else." She squeezed her eyes shut and rested her forehead against her hand. "Brit, how am I going to do this? I can't imagine living there without her."

"So you'll live here."

"Here?" The impulsive offer caught Paige off guard, but she felt her heart leap with hope and the dread that had been ramping up began to subside. "Do you really mean it?"

Brittany reached out and gave Paige's arm a pat. "Of course I mean it. I have an extra bedroom that you can stay in for as long as you need. We'll drive back to your place after Thanksgiving and pack up your things."

"Thanksgiving!" Paige's eyes widened in sudden horror. "I forgot all about it! I have to call my mom.

My entire family is expecting a huge feast the day after tomorrow, and I don't even have a table to put it on."

"Thanks to Veronica." For once, Paige wasn't going to argue with the judgment in her friend's tone.

"Oh, shit. The turkey!" An image of a giant thawing poultry made Paige's heart sink. "It's still sitting out to thaw. After everything else, it would break my heart for it to go to waste. I guess I'd better call Veronica and see if her mom wants to cook it for their dinner."

"Oh, hell no!"

"What?" Paige took in her friend's incensed face with surprise. "You said yourself that I won't get back to San Francisco until after Thanksgiving, and Veronica's family lives in the city."

Brittany tapped her manicured nails against the table and Paige could almost hear the whirring of her brain at work. "How much longer can it sit out?"

"Well, I packed it in ice, so tomorrow afternoon? That's when I was planning to put it in the apple cider brine." Paige blinked back tears as she recalled the mouthwatering recipes she'd selected with such care for their meal. She was a good cook, and this was to have been her moment of culinary triumph. Instead, she'd be lucky to have a frozen turkey dinner to heat up in the microwave. "I had fresh pumpkins for pie, too."

"*Fresh* pumpkin pie? That settles it. We'll go in the

morning." Brittany took a last swig of coffee and grabbed her briefcase.

"Go where?"

"Your apartment. The governor's office is holding a press conference this afternoon, so I have to go in today, but I'll take tomorrow off. The office usually closes at noon before a holiday, anyway. We're driving to San Francisco and bringing back that turkey, the pie fixings, and anything else that's still good. Then we're calling your family and telling them that dinner's at my house this year."

"Are you sure?" Paige couldn't help but laugh at Brittany's determination to save the day, but hosting a family dinner at a moment's notice was going above and beyond, even for a best friend.

"I didn't have any other plans, anyway," Brittany responded with a shrug. "And I'll be damned if a single member of Veronica's family is going to get one bite of that turkey. Or that heavenly pie."

After Brittany left for work, Paige tried to focus on the sense of calm that floated across the surface of her consciousness. She had a roof over her head that she could afford and her basic needs were accounted for. She knew she should feel grateful and relieved. And she did. But beneath that was a nothingness that terrified her, a numb tingling surrounding the part of her that had been torn open and ripped apart by Veronica leaving. She hadn't even begun to process it. Now that her most immediate worries had been resolved, the anesthesia of shock would wear off soon enough.

For years, Paige had built her world around Veronica. She'd been willing to change her own dreams at every turn in order to be what Veronica wanted. She'd done it for them, for their future. When it came to Veronica, she'd believed in forever. That faith was shattered now. There was a sneaking fear that when she took a good, hard look, she'd have no idea how to pick up the pieces.

TWO

I WON IT ALL! Fiona took a deep breath as the thrill of victory coursed through her. Her body trembled, giddily uncertain whether to laugh or cry. It was the same feeling she'd had on stage as her voice soared to its final note. The applause of the audience still thundered in her chest. It had been the culmination of a decade of work, and she'd known even as the last note still echoed from the rafters that she'd delivered the performance of a lifetime.

Fiona slid open the glass door to the balcony of her hotel room and stepped into the humid night air. It was the end of November, and though already well into winter's bitter cold and dreariness back home, the weather in Sydney was pleasantly warm as summer approached. Fiona drank it in as she looked out across the harbor to where the iconic Opera House glowed like a fleet of white-sailed ships in the night.

I have to call Alice. Fiona wanted to see her girlfriend's face when she told her, especially the bit about the prize money. She grabbed her phone, her stomach fluttering nervously as she selected the video call option. With a centuries-old farmhouse literally falling down around their heads, an infusion of cash would be welcome news. She would try to keep the conversation focused on that, and away from the likelihood that she'd now have performance opportunities pouring in from around the globe to keep her away from home even more than before.

"Alice!" A grin split Fiona's face as Alice's blond pixie-cut hair and ruddy cheeks came into view. "Guess what!"

"Fee! Oh thank God." A harried-looking Alice paused to brush her tangled hair from her face with a gloved hand, leaving a smear of dirt across her forehead. It looked ridiculous, but Fiona knew better than to laugh when Alice looked this stressed. "I'm losing my mind here. There's another break in the fence and all the sheep got out overnight. I've spent the entire morning rounding them up on my own. Please tell me you're coming home soon!"

"Oh dear." A wave of guilt surged over her as Fiona regarded Alice's tired face. "And Dolly didn't help at all to keep them in?"

"Dolly?" The name came out with a derisive snort. "Your brother's *guard llama* is as useless as he is."

"What, you mean Daniel's not there either?"

Annoyance flared up inside. She'd been counting on her brother's presence to lessen the stress of her latest absence. "But he promised to take the Friday evening train from Oxford as soon as classes got out!"

"Oh, his lordship's here, alright." Alice rolled her eyes. "But his bespoke boots and £600 shooting jacket aren't exactly practical for mending a fence."

"Oh dear," she said again. There wasn't much else to say. It was entirely her fault. When Alice's father had passed away unexpectedly the previous year, Fiona and her brother had taken the opportunity to tour Yorkshire while Alice met with the solicitors about her inheritance. It honestly hadn't occurred to either of them at the time that real farmers didn't wear the type of clothing that came from incredibly posh shops dedicated to outfitting country squires for weekend hunting trips. For the sake of her relationship, she'd had the good sense to put her own purchases in the back of the wardrobe where they could never again see the light of day, but Daniel hadn't shown similar wisdom. "He's not getting in the way too much, is he?"

"I've sent him off to give Dolly a walk so that Maxine can do her job." At the sound of her name, Maxine gave a loud bark off-screen. Alice's little border collie was a natural sheep herder, but she would only work when Dolly was nowhere in sight. The idea of a guard llama had sounded so innovative when she and Daniel had come across it online, but apparently the fact that dogs and llamas were natural enemies was just one of many reasons that guard llamas weren't already a staple on every sheep farm in the Holme Valley. It was one more thing about country living that Fiona hadn't known, one more thorn in Alice's side.

"Oh, Alice. I'm really sorry. I know I was supposed to be there to help, and instead I've missed the whole breeding season, plus this latest fence fiasco." Fiona sighed heavily. As excited as she'd been for the opportunity to compete in Sydney, she hated that it had meant letting Alice down again. It was getting to be a habit with her these days.

"Don't be silly, love. I know you couldn't pass this up." Alice's eyes squinted at Fiona through the screen, as if only just now taking her in. "Don't you look nice! I guess you're all ready for tonight's competition?"

Fiona touched her fingers to her jet black hair, which was still pulled up in an elegant chignon. "You've forgotten the time difference, darling. It's almost midnight here. It's already happened."

"Midnight?" A stricken look passed Alice's face at the realization. "Here I am blathering on about the sheep and not once asking how it went! So, how did you do?"

"I won!" The news she'd held back throughout Alice's rant exploded with geyser-like force.

"Oh, that's fantastic! So which prize did you get? Not just the one with the watch, I hope. Not that a watch isn't a nice prize, but a few pounds toward a new fence would be so much better."

"Well, in fact, I *did* get the watch. And also the grand prize, and the audience prize, and a few others, too." She laughed at the look of shock on Alice's face. She could hardly take offense. Even Fiona had never expected to do as well as she had. "It's over £50,000, darling!"

"£50,000?" Alice's jaw dropped, her face twisting into a painful grimace.

"Alice? Are you alright?" Fiona's body tensed in alarm. She knew the money would be a shock, but Alice's expression was all wrong.

Alice took a deep, ragged breath. "Yeah, sorry. It's nothing, just a pain in my side from rounding up the blasted sheep."

"Are you sure?" Fiona frowned. "You had the same thing happen last month. Don't you think it's time to give Dr. Ross a call?"

Alice waved the suggestion off with her free hand. "Who has time for that?"

"You will, as soon as you let Brandon know we need him as full-time caretaker for the farm."

"We can't afford that! Anyway, I'll be fine as soon as I take a paracetamol or two."

"£50,000, Alice, remember? I want you to let Brandon know today that we'll take him for as many hours as he can spare, starting immediately." Brandon had been the farm's caretaker when Alice's father was alive, but because of Alice's stubborn determination to run the farm herself, they'd cut his hours back to a minimum over the past year. It was obvious to Fiona from her girlfriend's recent fatigue and aching body that this had been a mistake. "And then call on Dr. Ross. No waiting until I get back, you hear me?"

"Fine," Alice replied with an exaggerated sigh. "Speaking of coming back, love, when *do* you expect to be home?"

"Soon. I'll need to stay a few extra days for the publicity tour, but after that I'll be home. Another week at the most."

"You'd better not be longer than that. The Christmas parade and tree lighting is the weekend after next." Alice's brow creased with worry. "You've missed it every year, and you promised to be back for it this time. You *can't* celebrate Christmas all alone in a foreign place where they string lights on palm trees, or whatever it is they do down there."

"I wouldn't miss a proper Yorkshire Christmas for anything!" Fiona tried to stifle a yawn, but the excitement of the day had drained the last drop of energy from her. "Sorry, darling. I'm completely knackered. We'll talk tomorrow?"

"Of course. Get some sleep! I love you!"

"Love you, too."

Fiona detected another flicker of pain on Alice's face as the video cut out, and a fresh stab of guilt hit her. Her girlfriend's stubbornness was only part of the reason she'd been working without a caretaker for so long. As their savings accounts dwindled and the bills stacked up, Fiona was constantly reminded that a full-time singing career didn't necessarily bring in a reliable wage. That's why this victory was so important. Between the prize money and future performances, their financial outlook was drastically improved. But it wasn't just about the money. For Fiona, it was even more valuable to have the certainty that the dream she'd worked for her entire adult life hadn't been the waste of time that she'd begun to fear it was. Of course, it was at odds with the simple farm life Alice envisioned for the both of them, but that was a problem for another day.

Giving in to another yawn, Fiona made her way back inside. Her room was no longer the cramped space without a view that she'd shared with another contestant in the days leading up to the competition. The hotel had relocated her to the spacious winner's suite immediately upon her return. She now occupied a massive room with an expansive view of the harbor, a room fit for a star.

Fiona giggled as it struck her that's exactly what she was. Fans had already been queuing up for autographs and selfies as she left the concert hall. The seating area in her suite promised to be filled to capacity in the morning with agents vying for her time and attention. Philip, her manager, had already been lining up the appointments as she stepped into the limo for the ride back to the hotel. The whole thing still felt like a dream. *It's a dream I could get used to, that's for certain!*

Fiona had never lacked confidence in her talent. In fact, she'd headed into the national competition in London over the summer positive she'd come in first place, just as she always had before in everything she did. She'd been top of her class at the Guildhall School, then chosen for the prestigious artist in residence program with the Royal Opera. When it came to her singing, succeeding was what she did. The move to the farm had been a distraction and she'd had to take time off from her rigorous vocal training, but she hadn't thought it would hurt her as much as it had. But then she'd placed third in a competition where only the top two could advance.

Coming so far just to lose by a hair's breadth had been a crushing blow. For the first time in her career, she'd had to admit to the possibility that raising sheep in West Yorkshire wasn't just a peripheral aspect of her life, but it's entirety. Without an alternative, she'd struggled to resign herself to her fate.

The first week of November, she'd received the call that changed everything. The second place winner had been disqualified, and Fiona was going to Sydney. With only a week to prepare, she knew better than to expect too much. Coming in third had taught her that lesson. She'd gone into this final leg of the competition simply hoping to do well enough to find some regional success that would guarantee some opportunities close to home. It was the perfect solution, a compromise that would allow her to live on the farm without losing her identity as a performer and going stark raving mad as a result.

She slid between the crisp, cold sheets and stretched her arms wide, and for a moment thought how nice it would be to be able to reach out and feel Alice's warm body beside hers. This was the hardest part about being away from home. She'd probably be away a lot more in the future, if her manager had his way. She sighed. Her new prospects were thrilling, but deep down she wished that Alice could get away from the farm and come with her. She loved Alice dearly, but at times like this, it struck her how nice it would be if they had more of their daily interests in common.

She'd just drifted into a light sleep when the screen of her phone lit the room with an incoming message, startling her awake. She squinted to make it out, the light hurting her eyes. It was a text from Philip. As Fiona read, her pulse quickened. *The New Year's Eve Gala?* She read it through again, just to confirm what she had seen. Was she actually being asked to sing at Sydney's world famous New Year's Eve celebration? *This is*—honestly, Fiona didn't have any words to describe what this was. An honor beyond belief? An opportunity only a fool would pass up? Nothing she could think to say would do it justice, so she simply typed "YES!!!" by way of reply, then set the phone back down on her nightstand. She closed her eyes again, but sleep was elusive.

Alice is going to kill me. Her already-racing heart ticked even faster as reality set in. With a show just days after Christmas, there was no way she could go home. Making the twenty-two hour flight twice in a matter of weeks was impractical. She knew Alice wouldn't be happy, but they could celebrate another time, maybe take a weekend holiday together in January.

Someplace warm, she thought with a smile teasing her lips. Warm weather might seem the antithesis of Christmas to a dyed-in-the-wool Yorkshire native like Alice, but Fiona, whose father was in the British Diplomatic Service, had spent much of her childhood in warmer climes. Grilled shellfish and a swim in the ocean were as much a part of the holiday as mincemeat and sleigh rides. Though she was loathe to admit it, spending the holiday in Sydney held a certain appeal.

Fiona grabbed her phone again and composed an email to explain the situation. It felt safer than a text. Alice read texts right away, but an email could sit for a while, if only long enough for Fiona to turn off the ringer and move the phone to another room until morning. Then she could sleep, and maybe the perfect way to placate Alice would come to her in a dream.

IT WASN'T until well into the morning that Fiona thought to look at her phone again. She'd awoken early to the sound of Philip banging on the door. He'd brought along a frightfully long list of morning appointments that put Fiona's stomach in knots, but he'd also brought an assistant to help get her ready and a very large mug of tea, so he was forgiven. Plus, the potential opportunities he'd lined up were beyond belief. The New Year's Eve Gala was just the tip of the iceberg. He was proposing a world tour, and recording contracts, besides. If Philip had his way, everyone on earth would know her name by this time next year!

It was in a quiet moment between meetings that Fiona picked up her phone. She cringed to see that she had half a dozen missed calls. Alice hated the phone. She must be even angrier than Fiona had thought if she was resorting to calling. *I'd better call her back.* Her finger was poised above the screen when she remembered the time difference. It was late evening in Yorkshire and well past when Alice usually went to bed. She was just setting the phone back down when it began to vibrate with an incoming call, and the shock of it made her jump and sent the phone careening across the table and onto the floor. She could see Alice's avatar on the lit screen as she got down on all fours to retrieve it. She just managed to stretch her arm as far as it would reach and hit the speakerphone button with the tip of her little finger before the call was sent to voicemail.

"Alice?" Fiona grunted as she tried once more to grab the phone. Her body tensed as she awaited Alice's tirade, but there was nothing coming from the phone but a murmuring too low to understand. "Hello, Alice?"

"*Fee?*"

Fiona frowned as her brother's voice came through the speaker. "Daniel? Why are you calling from Alice's phone?" There was more unintelligible murmuring in response. "Hold on, let me get this off speaker. You sound like you're in a tunnel." She gave a final stretch to retrieve the phone, then held it to her ear. "Start over, please?"

"*Sorry, the waiting room is noisy but I couldn't find a quieter place to call.*"

"Waiting room? Where are you?"

"*They've sent us on to St James' Hospital. They're prepping for surgery now.*"

"Hospital? Surgery?" Confused, Fiona cringed at the unpleasant words, though she couldn't think of anyone who was meant to be having surgery. One of Alice's cousins, perhaps? Several of them lived nearby. "*Who* are we talking about, Daniel?"

"*Alice.*"

Fiona's chest collapsed, trapping her breath in her lungs. She could barely force enough of it out to whisper back, "Alice?"

"*God, Fee, didn't you listen to your messages?*"

No, I didn't listen to my messages! She'd believed them

to be a collection of uncomfortable if well-deserved lectures about what a terrible Scrooge she was to ruin her girlfriend's favorite holiday. It wasn't that she was avoiding them so much as she was...*Okay, I was avoiding them.*

"I knew that pain was more serious than she let on." Fiona tried to let her satisfaction at being right blunt the sharpness of her guilt, with mixed success. *If I were really so bloody smart about it, I would have made her go to the doctor a month ago.*

"The pain got pretty bad after she talked to you, so I drove her to Dr. Ross. He sent her to Huddersfield for tests, and then they sent us on to Leeds."

"Thank you, Daniel, for taking care of her." *On my behalf because I'm a terrible girlfriend*, she added in her mind. "So, what was it, then, a hernia? Oh, not a slipped disk, I hope." Alice would be furious over that. It would put her out of commission for months.

"They're not entirely certain."

"They're not entirely—how can they operate if they don't know what they're operating on?"

"They know what's causing it, darling." His voice was gentle. "Just not what it is. There were, uh, spots."

"Spots? Like a rash?"

"Spots on the films. Tumors, Fee. They think it might be cancer."

Cancer? With trembling fingers, Fiona ended the call and stared at Alice's smiling avatar. Surely it couldn't be *cancer*. Just thinking the word hit her like a physical blow. Fiona needed to be home. Her pulse quickened as she thought about having to explain this sudden change of plans to Philip. He was even more ambitious than she was and she dreaded breaking the news, but it would have to be done.

Fiona rose from the sofa and strode resolutely to her room to pack her bag. *I've been selfish,* she thought as she stuffed rumpled clothing into her suitcase. *What was I thinking, staying in Sydney for Christmas?* She'd go home, and nurse Alice back to health. It would all turn out just fine, she was certain. Alice was young and healthy, and it was just a matter of time before she was back on her feet again. She'd learn to be a better girlfriend in the process, find a way to balance her priorities. When the new year arrived, she'd be ready to take the world by storm once more.

THREE

"THERE YOU ARE, MAXIE!" Soggy yellow and brown leaves squished beneath her wellies as Fiona traversed the deserted churchyard. November had rolled in with a bitter cold front, and her breath came out in frozen puffs in the damp air. A furry black and white head peaked out from behind a headstone, her own breath rolling in misty pants from her pink tongue. "Naughty puppy. How many times am I going to have to drag you home from here?" Maxine whimpered in response.

As Fiona reached down to scratch behind the dog's ears, she studiously avoided reading the words on the stone. There was no need. She knew well enough that Alice was gone without having to see her name in the white marble slab. Besides, she hated the headstone with its overly-precious carving of a little lamb at the top. Alice's cousins had chosen it, and offered her no say in the matter. And so Alice rested for eternity under a stone that proclaimed her as a beloved daughter and cousin, but made no mention of her role in Fiona's life at all. Of her many regrets, that one cut the deepest.

In a safe deposit box in London sat a sparkling sapphire in an antique platinum setting. Fiona's grandfather had given it to her grandmother, and she'd always known it was the ring she wanted to give to the woman she would spend her life with. She'd contemplated retrieving it several times during the years she and Alice were together, but for one reason or another she'd always put it off. Standing in the hospital room in Leeds, she'd promised Alice that they'd go fetch it together just as soon as she woke. Only Alice never did. In the end, the cancer had only needed a week to take her, and she never regained consciousness to hear Fiona's promise, or to say goodbye.

Fighting back the memory, Fiona brushed the wet leaves aside and tucked her coat beneath her as she sat on the bare ground, her back resting against the stone she refused to acknowledge. With a wag of her tail, Maxine hopped onto her lap and settled in with her head resting on muddy paws atop Fiona's trousers. Fiona pressed her head against the cold marble behind her, closing her eyes to hold back hot tears. Maxine stiffened suddenly, her body vibrating against Fiona's legs with a throaty growl. Fiona's eyes flew open, and she snorted derisively at the little dog as the source of her distress became clear. The white head of a llama peaked over the stone wall surrounding the churchyard, and Maxine's growl intensified.

"After all that we've been through this year, you still can't get along?" Fiona heard the squeak of hinges from the iron gate and sighed as she saw her brother approach.

"I thought I'd find you here." Daniel's brow was deeply creased, and Fiona knew he found her frequent visits to Alice's grave concerning.

"It wasn't my doing this time, I swear. I just came to find the dog." Her excuse was made less plausible by the fact that the border collie had disappeared behind the headstone at the first sounds of her brother's approach. It wasn't just Dollie that Maxine objected to these days. Since Alice's death, she had little use for anyone.

"Well, I'm glad I ran across you. I was just heading out to check the fences. Want to join me?" Daniel's hopeful smile gave Fiona's heart an uncomfortable twist.

"I don't know..." She knew she should. It was her farm now, after all, and her responsibility. But she just felt too tired most of the time to make an effort.

"You could come talk to Brandon about how the breeding season is going?"

"I'm sure it's fine. Brandon knows what he's doing."

"The food orders need to be placed for the Black

Fleece, and Maria was hoping to go over some ideas she had for menu changes before Christmas."

Fiona groaned heartily at that. She'd been meaning to meet with Brandon's wife, Maria, for weeks. Maria was the cook at the little pub that sat at the edge of the farm's property. Somehow she just hadn't found the energy for that, either. "Maybe we can just keep the menu the same for this month, and talk about the changes before the next order?"

"Fee, business at the Black Fleece is down twenty percent since last year. If we don't make some changes and take advantage of the Christmas rush, we won't be able to cover the expenses much longer."

"I know, but—"

"Do you, Fee? Do you *really* know?" Daniel's voice straddled the line between tenderness and exasperation. He brushed a pile of leaves aside with his foot and settled onto the ground beside Fiona. "I know it's hard, darling, but this is your responsibility now."

"I just need some time."

"It's been a *year*. Brandon's been keeping the farm going, and Maria's got the day-to-day running of the tavern mostly in hand, but there are decisions that need to be made that only you can make. They're not the owners. Neither am I."

"You've been doing a great job, Daniel. I really appreciate it." Daniel had been her rock since taking a leave of absence from school and moving to Yorkshire full time to help out. She didn't know how she would have made it through without him.

"Yeah, but this isn't permanent, Fee. I'm interested in international policy, not agriculture. And I need to get back to my studies."

"My studious little brother, following in Dad's footsteps." She reached out and gave him a playful pinch on the chin. "But you've just fixed up your cottage so nicely, Daniel. What's the hurry to leave?" The prospect of her brother heading back to Oxford at the start of the new term in mid-January filled her belly with cold dread. *If only he could be persuaded to push it off until April, or maybe next October, I know I'll be ready by then.*

"This isn't my home. It isn't my life."

What, like it's mine? She wanted to shout it out, but even before the words could leave her mouth, Fiona realized her error. Whether it felt like it or not, this *was* her home, and her life. *My lonely home and empty life.* A tear escaped her eye and rolled down her cheek as Daniel's warm hand came to rest on her shoulder.

"If it isn't what you want, why don't you leave? Any one of Alice's cousins would be happy to offer you a fair price for the farm. Liam's just about begging for the place. Sell it to him and go back to London. See your friends again. Get in touch with Philip and get back to your singing career."

Fiona shook her head, as she had every time the

subject had been broached during the past year. "I've told you before, I'm done with singing." She could feel her throat closing up as she spoke. She would never forgive herself for being away when Alice needed her most, for putting her career first. The loss of her voice was her penance. She wanted nothing to do with music anymore. "As for selling the farm, Alice trusted me with this place. *Me*. Not Liam or the rest of the cousins. I can't just leave it."

"Then you need to start running it, Fee."

She sighed, the weight of that truth pressing down on her. "First thing tomorrow, I'll go see Brandon, then stop in to talk to Maria. I promise. Does that make you happy?"

"It's a start. You need to snap out of this funk you're in and start taking an interest. Maybe even think about dating again, eventually?"

Fiona rolled her eyes in response. That wasn't going to happen. The valley was hardly a hotbed of lesbian nightlife, and even if she met someone, she wasn't cut out for love. She'd been a monumental failure as a partner when Alice needed her most. That was proof enough that she was better off alone.

"You don't want to be by yourself forever."

Don't I? Perhaps not, but it was her destiny, not that she knew how to explain that to him. She slumped against her brother's shoulder and attempted to lighten the mood. She sighed dramatically. "Alright, you win. Next time a hot lesbian wanders into the Black Fleece, I'll snap her right up. I promise." Since it would never happen, she felt confident that was at least one promise she could keep.

Daniel laughed as he kissed her on the temple. "That's my girl."

A LOUD TAPPING roused Fiona from her sleep, and she sat up groggily, not entirely certain where she was. Rubbing her eyes, she slowly recognized the shabby farmhouse living room that surrounded her as being her own, and she had a vague recollection of curling up with a bottle of her favorite Irish whiskey as a nightcap after her walk home from the churchyard. The half-empty bottle next to the couch suggested that she'd had more than one, which was a little bit troubling. It wasn't a regular occurrence, but it wasn't the first time, either, since Alice's death. The bright light streaming through the windows hinted that she'd slept there through the night, and that it was now well into the next day. The tapping came again, louder this time, from the direction of her front door.

"Fiona?" Daniel's voice pierced the heavy wooden door and lodged in her skull.

After a quick glance to confirm that she was fully dressed, albeit in yesterday's clothing, Fiona opened the door. "Hi, Daniel. What brings you around this early?" Her voice was filled with a forced brightness she didn't feel.

"It's noon."

Fiona winced. She'd had no idea what the time was, but she'd been praying for something a little closer to ten. "I was just heading down to talk to Brandon right now."

"Oh, were you?" He eyed the top of her head in a quizzical manner that told Fiona that whatever her hair was doing at the moment, it wasn't pretty. And Daniel wasn't fooled. "He had to run errands in town, which you would know if you'd at least tried to see him this morning like you promised."

"I'm sorry, Danny. The truth is, I had a hard time sleeping last night and needed some extra time this morning." The truth was, she'd drunk too much and then slept like a log for eighteen hours straight, but that wasn't likely to garner as much sympathy.

"Right. Why don't you go fix that mop on your head and then we'll walk down to the Black Fleece to see Maria. Together."

Standing at the bathroom sink, Fiona blinked several times at her reflection in the mirror. *When did I let myself get like this?* A year ago, she'd looked like a star. The gaunt, disheveled woman who looked back at her now was hardly recognizable. Recalling the deal she'd made with Daniel, Fiona could only shake her head. It was probably for the best that she never planned to date again. One look at her like this and any potential girlfriend would go running in the opposite direction.

She stared helplessly at the basket of brushes, combs, and hair products. It was no use. This was a job for a professional. With a silent vow to book an appointment at the salon in Holmfirth as soon as she could, she fished a tweed cap from the back of a cabinet and pulled it down to cover the frizzy mess on her head, then swished a toothbrush around her mouth a few times, and declared the result good enough for now.

Daniel led the way from the stone farmhouse, along the gravel road past his own smaller cottage, and to the footpath that wound its way down the hill to the medieval village of Holme. The place was hardly large enough to merit a dot on a map, being little more more than a cluster of ancient stone buildings along the narrow road that looped through the valley by way of the much more substantial villages of Holmebridge and Holmefirth. It was possible to drive from one end of Holme to the other without realizing it was there, and people often did. The Black Fleece Inn was the only business within the village proper. It had offered both meals and lodging to travelers once upon a time, but the guest rooms were sorely outdated, even worse than the place as a whole, so now it just served as the local pub.

Fiona followed her brother inside, her stomach

rumbling as she breathed in the smell of roasting meat coming from the kitchen. At a few tables in front of the fireplace, local patrons sat eating lunch or nursing a pint of ale. Aside from that, the place was empty, though Fiona felt like there should have been more people than there were at that hour. Her brother's remark about declining sales flitted through her memory and an uneasiness spread through her. *Why hadn't I noticed this before?* As with the farm, the running of the tavern had been Alice's domain. Fiona had offered support and a helping hand, but Alice was the one with the brains for improving the business. *I'm not sure I can handle this on my own.*

Maria emerged from the kitchen with two bowls of soup and a basket of bread balanced on a tray. She was a bubbly young woman with a smiling face and long black hair caught up in a braid down her back. She had a sturdy, noticeably rounded frame that caught Fiona by surprise. She'd known that Brandon and Maria were expecting a baby of course, but she hadn't remembered her being *this* pregnant. With a sinking feeling, she realized that her cook's upcoming maternity leave was one more issue she would have to figure out.

Fiona sat at the table where Maria placed the tray, frowning as Daniel failed to follow suit. Instead, he grabbed a slice of bread from the basket and headed toward the door. "Danny, aren't you going to join us?"

He shook his head. "Nah, this is your meeting. I was just meant to get you here."

Fiona pushed her chair back from the table, her heart thudding erratically in her chest. "Daniel," she pulled up beside him, her voice low but urgent, "I *need* you here!"

"You're a big girl, Fee. You can do this on your own."

"No!" Her voice hitched with growing alarm. "I really want you to stay."

He closed his eyes, a pained expression marring his face. "I'll be waiting outside. Come and get me if you need me." The door closed behind him, and Fiona flinched at the sound of the latch clicking shut.

Alone with Maria, Fiona smiled nervously. Though as friendly as she could be on a personal level, Fiona found Maria's strict efficiency with anything concerning the kitchen or the menu beyond intimidating. She bought herself a few minutes by dipping her spoon into her steaming bowl and taking several bites. As the hearty soup reached her stomach, Fiona felt her nerves settle, and it occurred to her to wonder just how long it had been since she'd had a proper, hot meal. *How am I supposed to take care of this place if I can't take care of myself?* But after several more bites, Fiona's confidence was bolstered, and ultimately she got through the food order with minimal fuss, and promised to read through the menu proposals Maria had written up for her consideration.

"I told you you could do it," Daniel said when she joined him outside.

Fiona shrugged noncommittally. "I survived. I wouldn't say it was my most brilliant performance."

"But you did it, and that's the important thing. And in the morning, you'll talk to Brandon."

Fiona's face fell at the reminder. "Oh, Daniel. Can't you talk to him, just this once? You know the animals better than I do, anyway." She knew it was taking advantage to keep asking for his help, but she couldn't seem to stop herself, no matter how guilty it made her feel.

"I'm not always going to be here, Fee."

"I know, but you're here now! Please?"

They'd been walking back up the path as they talked, Fiona becoming increasingly petulant under Daniel's unrelenting tough love approach. Self-reliance, like bitter medicine, was easier in small quantities, and Fiona felt that she'd consumed a large enough dose for one day.

"We'll talk about this later, Fee." Daniel lifted the gate's latch and stepped into the front garden. Fiona could hear him muttering something about 'for your own good' as she continued along the lane.

As she reached her front door, she turned to give her brother's cottage a final glance and frowned. Daniel had his phone in one hand and was snapping photos as he walked the perimeter of the property. Fiona shook her head, puzzled by what he was doing. Her brother had an odd streak to him sometimes. The man had a pet llama, for heaven's sake. She loved him dearly and couldn't live without him, but sometimes his actions were beyond explanation. She shrugged and went into the house without giving it another thought. She had too many of her own problems to worry about.

FOUR

WITH A WHOOSH, the lid of the plastic container clicked shut beneath her fingers. All around her Paige could still smell the succulent aroma of homemade chicken soup. She'd added rosemary and a squeeze of lemon this time, her secret ingredients to combat colds and flu. *Poor Veronica.* She'd sounded terrible on the phone, her voice all hoarse and croaky. Some homemade soup was just what she needed.

Now to keep it hot for the drive. She dug around in the cupboard until she found a thermal bag large enough to fit the huge container of soup. As she lowered it in, she heard Brittany's key in the front door and froze. Her friend was home from work earlier than she'd expected. She eyed the soup guiltily. There would be no chance of ever explaining the situation to Brittany's satisfaction if she guessed what was going on. At the sound of footsteps entering the kitchen, Paige looked up with an expression as close to pure innocence as she could muster.

"I made some chicken soup."

"I can smell that!" Brittany took an exaggerated sniff. "That's fantastic! Should I get us some bowls?"

Paige bit her lip nervously. "No, none for me. I'm heading out to a gig."

"A gig? That's great news!" Brittany's eyes narrowed as she studied the large bag on the counter. "That's a lot of soup you're taking with you."

"This? It was the only thing I could find to keep it warm."

"What are you talking about?" Brittany frowned. "I have at least three lunch containers that are just meant for soup. In fact, I think your mother was the one who gave them to me."

"I didn't see them." Paige shrugged and grabbed the bag. "Gotta go!"

"Hold on a second." Paige paused mid step at the sternness in her friend's voice. "Where is this gig of yours."

"Uh, San Francisco?"

Brittany's eyes narrowed and her frown became a scowl. "Paige, be honest. Are you taking that soup to Veronica?"

"I...um..." Paige's shoulders slumped in defeat. "She has a cold."

"I knew it. Paige! Are you kidding me?"

"Look, I know what you're thinking, but I was

making the soup anyway, plus her place is on the way."

"Where *exactly* is this gig tonight?"

Paige mumbled the name of a bar that was decidedly not located anywhere near Veronica's apartment. "But it's *hardly* out of the way. And she thinks it might be strep throat."

"Paige, it has been almost a year since that woman broke up with you and crushed your spirit, and still she thinks she can just crook her little finger and you'll drop everything and come running. Clearly she's right. But she has an entire family living within minutes of her apartment, not to mention plenty of money to buy her own soup. Meanwhile you're working your ass off playing piano for tips in shitty bars and driving two hours each way on Saturdays to play the organ at a wedding chapel in Reno."

Paige stiffened defensively. "It's not uncommon for musicians to make extra cash playing weddings. It's a lucrative industry."

"Sure, if you're playing receptions, maybe. But you work in a tacky chapel with red velvet curtains that's run by an Elvis impersonator. Not even hot, sexy Elvis. You're plunking out 'Here Comes the Bride' twenty times a day on a cheap electric organ for goddamn *peanut-butter-and-banana* Elvis."

Tears stung the corners of Paige's eyes. "I'm just trying to find my footing, okay?"

"By bringing Her Majesty homemade chicken *soup*?"

Paige grimaced. When Brittany said it, it sounded so much less reasonable than it did in her head. "Veronica's important to me."

"I know she is, sweetie." Brittany closed her eyes and drew in a deep breath. "I just wish you were as important to her. She uses you, Paige. She may not even know she's doing it, but she strings you along, and you fall for it every time. You'll never move on this way."

Paige sighed. Everything Brittany had just said was true, and deep down she knew it. She just didn't know how to fix it. Veronica had a hold over her that she couldn't explain. It had been like that since the day they'd met. No matter how obvious it was that Veronica didn't share her feelings, Paige couldn't shake the belief that if she just waited patiently, her ex would change her mind. It's what had kept her going for most of the past year, even as her career and living situation became less and less ideal.

Pulling up a chair, Paige joined her friend at the kitchen table. "I don't know what to do, Brit. This isn't the way my life's supposed to be. I mean, by twenty-seven, I at least thought I'd have my own place. No offense."

"None taken." Brittany patted her hand. "Look, I love having you here. How could I not?" She gestured around the cheery kitchen with one hand. "In the year that you've been my roommate, you've turned my dull condo into a cozy home. You've got a real knack for decorating. Not to mention cooking. I've gained at least ten pounds! You're quite the good wife, actually."

"Veronica didn't think so," Paige said sullenly.

"Well, Veronica's an idiot. The point is, though, as much as I enjoy having you live here, maybe it's time you thought about going somewhere else. Somewhere far away from Veronica."

"Come on, Brit. Where would I go?"

"What about that friend of yours in Los Angeles who does the indie films. Didn't he want you to do the score for one of them?"

"Mike? Yeah, he's got a project he was hoping I could take on, but I doubt it pays much. I don't have enough experience to land anything permanent in LA."

"It would be a great résumé builder, though, right? If you did the score for his film, it might lead to something bigger. Southern California could be the perfect place for you."

"Sure, but I kinda still need to make money to pay rent in the meantime."

Brittany's face softened in thought. "What if you didn't have to?"

"Didn't have to pay rent?" Paige shook her head. "No way, Brit. I couldn't live here and not pay. I won't take advantage of you."

"No, not here. And not permanently. I just thought

of this, so it might still be a little half-baked, but hear me out, okay?"

"Okay." Her brow wrinkled as she tried to figure out where this was going.

"There's this article I was reading, about a company that helps arrange house swaps. It's mostly, like, academics and creative types who want a cheap way to visit another city or country for a month or two during semester breaks or for a sabbatical."

"Another country?" Paige couldn't help feeling intrigued. With the exception of trips to see her grandparents in Minnesota, she'd rarely left California. "But what would I swap? It's not like I have a house of my own."

"They could stay in your room here, and since I wouldn't charge you rent for the time you were away, you could afford to go."

"I'll admit, it's tempting." Paige felt a flutter of hope in her chest. "But you wouldn't mind having a stranger living here?"

"It could be fun! Anyway, I'd help you look at the listings so we find someone I feel comfortable with."

"If I had a quiet place to work for a couple of months and wasn't always running from gig to gig, I could easily finish that film score for Mike—"

"And there would be no more working at the Velvet Elvis."

Paige laughed. "That's incentive enough, right there!"

"And maybe if you're far enough away from Veronica that she can't keep you at her beck and call, you can finally get her out of your system for good."

"Maybe." The smile on Paige's face faded to a somber line as she contemplated that prospect. She wasn't even certain she knew who she'd be if Veronica were no longer part of the equation. She'd already tried for a year to figure it out, and had failed miserably. Could something as simple as distance really be the key?

Brittany patted her hand again, giving her fingers a squeeze. "Okay, then. It's settled. We'll take a look at that website together in the morning and see what we can find. Right now, you need to run off to that gig of yours and make some money to pay your evil landlord."

Paige chewed her lip as she studied the swirls of color on the Formica tabletop. "About that gig. I have a confession. It's less of a paying gig and more of an open mike night. I was just using it as an excuse to go into the city to see Veronica."

"Oh, Paige. You see why you need to get away?"

"Because I was going to drive over an hour to play the piano for free just so I could bring soup to my ex?" A wave of disgust distorted Paige's features. "I'm really pathetic."

"Oh, sweetie, you're not pathetic."

"I packed an overnight bag just in case she wanted me to sleep on the couch."

"Okay, that's a little pathetic. For two hours of driving and your delicious homemade soup, you should have at least expected to get some friendly ex-sex out of it."

"Is that so? I hadn't thought of it that way. Maybe I should bring her the soup after all." Paige lost her struggle to keep a straight face as Brittany gave her shoulder a playful slug. "That was a joke, I promise!"

"Maybe you should dish up a couple bowls of that soup while I go grab my laptop. We've got house swaps to look at, and you're not going anywhere near Veronica's apartment tonight."

With the computer set up between them on the table, Brittany quickly found the website. But after browsing through options from just about every country on the planet, Paige soon felt overwhelmed. Head spinning, she pushed back against her chair and stared at the ceiling. "How do I choose? I don't even know where I want to go!"

"It's almost winter. How about someplace warm, like Brazil?"

Paige's eyes lit up with excitement. "Brazil! That's a great idea. They've got the music, and the good weather, plus all the food..." She'd pulled up a search for flights to Rio de Janeiro on her phone as she spoke, and the results filled her with dismay. "These flights are almost three thousand dollars, Brit. Even with free rent, I can't spend that much."

"How about Australia?"

Paige checked, then shook her head. "It's just as bad. Maybe Hawaii, though?"

Brittany pulled up the house swap page for Hawaii and frowned. "Everything for Hawaii is booked, and it looks like there's a waiting list."

"Damn. Okay, maybe someplace warm is unrealistic at this time of year. I'm going to check out that discount travel site and see what places I can actually afford." Paige cocked her head as she surveyed the list and a particularly good bargain caught her eye. "Can that be right? It says here there's a flight from San Francisco to London for three hundred bucks one way!"

With a grin, Brittany clicked on the house swaps for the UK. "Oh, there's a ton of choices, Paige! You know what, just thinking of the UK puts me in the mood for tea. You want to make a pot while I see if I can sort these to find the best options?"

Clearing their empty bowls from the table, Paige placed them in the kitchen sink, then filled the electric kettle with water and went on the hunt for tea. Every so often, her search was interrupted by a question from Brittany.

"Are you okay with just a shower, or do you want a tub, too?"

"Umm, probably a tub, too."

"What about laundry facilities?"

"Definitely." Paige located a tea bag and dropped it into a mug as the kettle clicked off.

"Well, finding something in London with all the amenities you're used to looks a little unlikely, but what about somewhere in the countryside?"

Paige handed Brittany a steaming mug and shrugged. "That could be nice, I guess."

Brittany frowned at the single mug. "Didn't you make any for yourself?"

"Not a fan of tea. So maybe England's not the best place for me, after all."

"I'm pretty sure they have coffee, too." Suddenly, Brittany's face lit up. "And you'll just have to risk it, because I found you the perfect place!"

"Oh?" Paige cocked an eyebrow expectantly.

"It's an adorable stone cottage in Yorkshire. It's available from now until just after the new year. Oh, and you won't believe this, but it has a piano!"

"Let me see." Paige tilted the laptop screen toward her for a better view. Sure enough, inside the charming old cottage was an upright piano that reminded her of the one she'd taken her first lessons on as a kid. "Well, that's a nice surprise! I wonder if it's been tuned..."

"We can always send a note to the owner to ask." Brittany flipped the laptop around to face her. "Oh, mama!"

Paige laughed at her friend's enthusiastic response to whatever new feature she'd discovered. "That sounds promising! What, does it have a hot tub or something?"

"Uh, something hot alright. Take a look at the

owner!" She spun the computer back around so that Paige could see. On the screen was a man of around thirty with jet black hair and olive skin. His facial hair was trimmed into a trendy goatee, and he wore what looked like a tweed hunting jacket.

Paige studied the picture for a moment, blinking. "I'll admit, he's not as pasty as I expected for an Englishman."

"Nope. Tall, dark, and handsome! He reminds me a little of that actor in *Hamilton*."

"Good God, is that an ascot around his neck?" Paige's eyes widened in mock-horror. "No wonder he reminds you of Hamilton. No one's worn ascots since the seventeen-hundreds." Paige giggled as Brittany glared at her from across the table. "Sorry, Brit, but it's not like he's *my* type."

"Yeah, well trust me, he's *mine*. And if I'm going to be sharing my house with this person for the next few months, I wouldn't mind getting some eye candy with the deal."

"Fair enough. So, I guess I'm going to Yorkshire." Paige felt a flutter in her belly as the reality of the statement hit her. *Am I really going to Yorkshire?*

Brittany let out a high-pitched *squee*. "This is so exciting! And if Yorkshire has men like this, maybe you'll find out they've got some attractive women, too."

"Well, you know what they say about Yorkshire women…" Paige waggled her eyebrows suggestively.

"No, what?"

"How the hell would I know, Brit?" Paige snorted. "I doubt I could find Yorkshire on a map! But the cottage looks comfortable, and the scenery's pretty. I'm sure I can get some work done there. Plus, it's six thousand miles away from Veronica."

"And that's really what it's all about. So, we're gonna do this?"

Paige closed her eyes and let the air drain slowly from her lungs. With her lids shut, she could see Veronica's face, just as she always could when she closed her eyes. Only it struck her now just how wrong that was, to be so wrapped up in a woman who would never love her the same way in return. Maybe things really would be better if she could learn to let her go.

"Yeah, we're gonna do this." She kept her eyes closed and listened to the clicking of the keyboard as Brittany filled out the required forms. If all went according to plan, she could be on her way to Yorkshire by this time next week.

FIVE

WHY DOESN'T anything ever go according to plan?

Paige stared at the man behind the counter and blinked, uncomprehending. "What do you mean the machine is out of order?"

Her flight from San Francisco had arrived at Gatwick airport an hour late, which is to say at precisely the same time as at least a dozen other international flights. The line for passport control had been a desperate mass of exhausted, unwashed humanity. By the time she emerged, luggage in hand, into the hallway that led to the train station, the clocks informed her that it was nearly eleven. Her weary body, deprived of sleep on the trans-Atlantic flight, told her it couldn't go another step without something stronger than the pale golden liquid that had passed for coffee on the plane. The glossy, full-color poster advertising a tall, steaming Caffè Americano at the coffee stand next to the entrance to the Gatwick Express had called to her like a beacon of hope. Only now her hopes seemed destined to be dashed.

"It isn't working," explained the man behind the counter. "I'm very sorry for the inconvenience. Can I get you some tea instead?"

Paige shook her head, biting her tongue to avoid insulting the national beverage, and headed toward the train empty-handed. A rumbling in her belly belatedly reminded her that she should have at least grabbed a pastry. Fortunately, it was only a half an hour by train into Victoria Station, and a quick Tube ride from there to King's Cross where she would catch a train to the Yorkshire town of Huddersfield. She knew from her research that the train would have some sort of dining facilities, so she resolved to tamp down all thoughts of coffee and food until she was safely on board.

Thirty minutes later, Paige found herself in front of a sign blocking the entrance to the Victoria Station underground, a sign which apologized profusely for the inconvenience of a one-day Tube strike. It was, she mused, at least the second apology she'd received already that day. While her track record for things going according to plan was getting worse by the minute, she had to admit that so far, this country was very good at apologizing about it.

With an under-caffeinated sigh, Paige rolled her suitcase into a line for the information booth that rivaled the one she'd stood in for passport control.

Lines and apologies. Britain excelled at both. *Are the trains to Yorkshire even running during the strike?* Paige twisted the corner of her shirttail between nervous fingers as she realized that she didn't have a clue.

As the line inched forward, Paige noticed an attractive woman working at the counter. Her pulse ticked faster and her first instinct was to look away as an image of Veronica filled her mind and demanded loyalty. *Not that she deserves any loyalty from me!* Just then, she caught a glimpse of her reflection in a nearby window, and was taken aback. *Damn, I look good!*

She might feel like just another clueless tourist suffering from a lack of coffee, but thanks to Brittany's insistence on a last minute shopping trip, at least she *looked* like a rock star. Her purple hair, freshly dyed to a luxurious eggplant hue, hung in thick braids on either side of her head. Her dark wool peacoat and short plaid skirt were right on trend, and the black suede knee-high boots that she wore atop a pair of cable-knit leggings were absolutely to die for. Defiantly, she swiveled her head back toward the information agent, and could have sworn that she'd just missed the woman staring at her with thinly-veiled interest.

"Next in line, please!"

Paige beamed a smile at the handsome agent, and felt a flush of pleasure as she realized that the woman was most definitely checking her out as she approached. *Veronica? Veronica who?* She was filled with a sense of adventure that verged on naughtiness. *What if instead of asking directions, I ask this woman out for dinner instead?* She stifled a giggle at her boldness.

"Can I help you?" the woman had asked in a low, sultry voice that turned Paige's insides to jelly.

"I need to get to King's Cross?" Paige cringed at her awkward mumbling, the antithesis of the confidence she'd hoped to project. In an instant, she'd become intensely aware of the difference between *looking* like a rock star and actually *being* one. Though the fact that she'd considered asking the woman out at all still counted as progress as far as she was concerned. That's what this trip was supposed to be all about, after all.

The agent grimaced and sucked in air between her teeth with a whistle. "Good luck to you." Possibly sensing Paige's rising panic, she added, "You *might* try a cab." The suggestion lacked conviction.

Paige attempted to remain hopeful. "Where would I find one?"

"That's the question of the hour, love." The agent chuckled a little as their eyes met, and Paige could feel a rush of heat coloring her cheeks at the whispered way that she said *love* in that dreamy British accent of hers. "Cabs and buses are hard to come by when there's a strike. Walking might be your best option." She handed Paige a tourist map, with a rough path marked in pencil, and winked as she did so in a way that buoyed Paige's spirits considerably as she headed out of the station.

Her excitement at finding herself in the heart of London carried her the several blocks between the station and Buckingham Palace. There, Paige stopped to take pictures of the palace guards with their famous red uniforms and black furry hats, and made a mental note to thank Brittany for pushing her to make the trip. There was a bounce in her step most of the way through St. James' Park, as well, as she soaked in the novelty of her surroundings. But by the time she limped closer to Trafalgar Square, her very stylish suede boots began to make it clear that they were not intended for extensive walking. And still there wasn't a cab or bus to be found that wasn't already crammed to capacity.

"Hop-on-hop-off-bus-tour, Miss?" A young man shoved a piece of paper into her hand. "See all the London sights!"

"The only sight I'm looking for right now is King's Cross Station. I don't suppose your bus stops there?"

The man nodded with enthusiasm. "Yes, of course!"

"Really? And I could find a seat and everything?" The last bus Paige had seen had been so full that two people were hanging out the open door as it drove past. She shuddered at the memory.

"Lots of seats, and you'll be at King's Cross in ten minutes!" With that assurance, Paige handed over two crisp twenty pound notes. It would have been a bargain at twice the price just to get off her aching feet.

A quick examination of the paper in her hand revealed a route map, where she discovered that King's Cross was on the yellow route. Or possibly the orange one. The quality of printing left something to be desired, and the two routes appeared identical in color. She turned to ask the young man, but he had already started talking to another potential customer. A yellow bus pulled up and, taking her best guess, she hopped on and sank into a seat near the door with a silent prayer of gratitude.

Unfortunately, her best guess was, as it turned out, wrong. The orange route would have been the correct choice, a fact which the driver confirmed for her after they'd gotten just far enough away from Trafalgar Square that the prospect of walking back brought tears to Paige's eyes. The buses only ran in one direction, making a loop. And so for the next two hours she snapped pictures of every major attraction in London, until the bus circled back to Trafalgar Square and she was able to transfer to the orange route for what really did turn out to be a ten-minute drive to King's Cross Station.

By now it was nearly four o'clock in the afternoon, and Paige was both starving and nearly delirious from her serious coffee deficiency. As she searched the screen in the middle of the station to find which track her train departed from, a delicious aroma tickled her nostrils. It came from a nearby stand, but as she contemplated exactly what manner of food a meat pasty was and tried to decide if she would enjoy one enough to wait in the endless line, her train was announced and the sudden rush of people toward the track convinced her that she should hurry to find a seat. She tightened the muscles around her stomach to minimize its complaining, and vowed to find the dining car as soon as she was able.

Just as soon as she'd found a seat and situated her suitcase for the journey, she went in search of a porter. "Excuse me?" she asked. "Where could I find some lunch?"

"Lunch?" The porter frowned. "It's after three."

Paige's brow creased to match the porter's. "But I haven't eaten anything today."

"Yes, well there aren't any dining services this late in the afternoon."

Her shoulders slumped at the unexpected news, and she could hear her stomach rumble loudly in protest. "None?"

"Just a tea trolley."

Oh, God. Not tea again! "I don't suppose it serves coffee, too?"

"Of course! And biscuits and crisps and the like. No worries, you won't starve."

Paige returned to her seat and waited for the trolley to come by. She ordered coffee and biscuits, and had to blink back tears of joy when the sugary smell of the little cookies wafted toward her from the opened package. She closed her eyes as she inhaled deeply and, upon opening her lids, was confused to discover that she was being offered the world's smallest coffee cup. For a moment she thought it might be a Christmas tree ornament. She cocked her head as she took it, pinched between two fingers, from the server's hand. It was a perfect replica of a normal paper cup, complete with a plastic lid with a hole for sipping, yet it was no more than two inches tall.

"What is this?" she asked, as some small part of her wondered if there was a joke she was missing. Maybe she was on the British version of Candid Camera?

"Espresso, Miss. We're out of Americano."

"Oh." Paige regarded the miniature cup for a moment, then popped off the lid and splashed the contents down her throat like a shot. *Fifteen more of these and I'll be all set!*

Feeling far from satisfied on all fronts, she closed her eyes and tried to imagine how differently her day might have gone if she'd had the courage to ask out that woman at the information desk. Assuming she had said yes—but why wouldn't she? I look fantastic!—they would have gone somewhere nice for dinner. *Maybe curry?* She'd heard that London was known for curry. Then back to the woman's apartment, perhaps? Paige blushed as she considered the finer points of what *that* part of the evening might have entailed. *Well, why not? I'm single, after all.* She'd never done anything like that before, just gone home with a stranger for the night and to hell with the consequences. But it was tempting in theory. Besides, it's not like she was naive enough to think relationships lasted forever anymore.

Anger bubbled in her chest. She'd spent so many years in love with Veronica that she didn't know where to begin in cataloging all the experiences she might have missed along the way. Her twenties were nearly over and her complete lack of scandalous sexual exploits was shocking. Though dating prospects in the Yorkshire countryside were likely to be slim, Paige vowed not to let future opportunities pass her by the way she had the woman at the train station. *Life's too short!*

When the train pulled into Huddersfield, Paige didn't feel the slightest bit surprised to find that the newsstand that sold sandwiches and snacks had closed for the night. She'd grown accustomed to her bad luck. She boarded the bus to Holme and told the driver the address of the cottage for good measure. She could only hope that there would be something in the cupboard when she arrived. Even a box of cereal would be welcome at this point.

It was a few minutes after nine o'clock when the bus pulled to a stop at the edge of a cluster of old stone buildings. He pointed up a dark gravel path and told her she'd find her cottage just up the hill. She watched the bus's red taillights disappear into the darkness, then shuffled along the empty road, pulling her suitcase behind her. She let out a quiet cheer when at last the little cottage appeared, but her joy was short lived. She'd expected to find the porch light on and a key beneath the mat. Instead the house was dark and there was no key in sight.

After trying the door twice for good measure, she accepted that it was bolted shut. Tears of frustration welled up, making her vision blur. With no other options, she trudged back down the hill to the tiny village. Most of the buildings were dark, but one was brightly lit. A small sign above the door declared it to be the Black Fleece Inn.

An inn! Relief flooded her, along with exhaustion. Her limbs protested with every ache they'd been accumulating over the trip. It had been twenty-four hours since her plane had left San Francisco, and Paige was dead on her feet. An inn meant she could rent a room for the night and figure out what to do about the cottage in the morning. As she pushed open the door, the smell of roasted meat greeted her with its mouth-watering goodness, and Paige was overjoyed to discover that the first floor of the inn was a restaurant. This time it was tears of happiness that welled up in her eyes.

"Good evening, Miss! Can I get you a pint?"

Paige smiled at the pretty, dark-haired woman who called out to her from behind the bar. "Maybe later. First I need some food."

"Oh, I'm sorry. The kitchen's already closed." Paige realized the expression on her face must have matched the desperation in her belly when the woman quickly added, "Let me see what I can find."

The bartender slipped through the door into the kitchen. As she did so, Paige noticed her swollen baby bump, and saw the look that passed between her and the only other patron in the inn, a strapping young farmer who sat at the edge of the bar. *I guess it's safe to assume she's not available,* Paige reasoned, though she wasn't certain why she was suddenly so focused on the issue. She'd been single for a year, but it was like the fact had only just occurred to her today. *I've been sizing up every woman I've seen since the plane landed at Gatwick!* Perhaps England really was beyond Veronica's sphere of influence, after all.

Paige looked around the cozy space and smiled tiredly. It was exactly the type of place she'd imagined in a Yorkshire village, with dark wooden tables and mismatched chairs, and a fire roaring in a fireplace against one end. With the exception of the bartender's gentleman friend, she appeared to be the only other human there, though a black and white dog with small, floppy ears dozed on a rug near the hearth. She set her suitcase and coat to one side and, spying a padded bench in the corner, Paige tucked herself into the nook and waited for the bartender to return.

As she settled in, the little dog opened its eyes and gave her an appraising look. It stood up, stretched its legs with a high-pitched whine, then moved beneath the table and curled into a ball at her feet. Paige reached down and gave it a scratch behind the ears, and was rewarded with a thumping of a tail against her boot. Paige chuckled. She may have chickened out on a sexy dinner date in London, but at least she seemed to have made a friend. Which wasn't to say that the next time a good looking woman crossed her path and showed some interest, she wouldn't try a little harder to make something come of it. But for now, canine companionship was an acceptable substitute.

A blast of chilly air caught Paige's attention as the door to the inn opened and a woman walked in. Paige felt her senses tingle as she watched the newcomer take long, confident strides toward the bar. Her dark, shoulder-length hair was tucked beneath a tweed cap, and she wore a matching tweed cape and beige equestrian-style pants so tight they appeared to have been painted onto her shapely thighs. Knee-high leather riding boots completed the country squire look. The only thing missing was her hunting dog. The heat that radiated from Paige's core rivaled that of the coal fire raging beside her, and she felt a sudden dizziness that mere lack of food couldn't explain.

The bartender had not yet returned, but this didn't deter the woman, who simply walked around to the other side of the counter and poured herself a pint. Paige gaped at her take-charge attitude, acting just as if she owned the place. What wasn't to like about a woman who knew what she wanted and took it? The lack of a bartender wouldn't stand in *that* woman's way, a quality that Paige found irresistibly attractive. She fanned herself unconsciously as she contemplated just how many other ways a woman like that might show similar boldness under the right circumstances. *Stripping off those boots, for starters, perhaps?*

The woman turned to look at her, and Paige felt her face flush scarlet. She turned her head quickly and pretended to busy herself by looking at the drinks menu, but she doubted she was fooling anyone. She might as well have been holding a neon sign confirming that she'd been picturing the woman naked. Embarrassment at her obviousness engulfed her. *What has gotten into me? I've turned into a horndog!*

Whether it was hunger, or exhaustion, or just the change of scenery Paige wasn't certain, but she couldn't remember the last time she'd felt so turned on by a stranger. The incident with the agent at the train station was insignificant by comparison. *Am I just getting desperate,* she wondered, *or is there something to this that I should explore?* Hazarding another glance at the woman, Paige's heart skipped a beat to find that she was being watched with what appeared to be keen interest in her gaze. *Or is that just wishful thinking on my part?* It's not like she was in San Francisco anymore. Did England even have a large enough LGBTQ population that she'd be likely to run into not one but *two* lesbians in the same day, just by chance? *I probably should have done more research into this...*

Maintaining eye contact, the stranger picked up

another glass and poured a second pint. With a glass in each hand, she walked toward Paige's table with a deliberateness that was unmistakable. Paige's pulse throbbed in her throat. This was it, that second chance she'd promised herself she wouldn't squander. With a rough swallow punctuating her suddenly shallow breathing, she watched as the stranger set the frothy beers onto her table and pulled out a chair.

SIX

HER BROTHER'S HASTILY SCRIBBLED note crackled in Fiona's hand as she balled it into a fist and shoved it into the pocket of her cape. *America?* How could having *him* go traipsing off for a six-week holiday in America possibly be for *her* own good? And he hadn't even had the courage to tell her in person that he was leaving. Instead, she'd come home from her day in Holmsfirth to find the note tucked beneath her front door, and Daniel already gone.

She marched down the hill toward the Black Fleece, past her brother's dark cottage, muttering under her breath the whole way. *The coward!* And after all the progress she'd made, too. Daniel had made his point about how she'd been living, or failing to live, for the past year loud and clear. It's not like she hadn't been listening. She'd booked a hair appointment, hadn't she? And poured the rest of the bottle of Jameson's down the sink, though she'd keep that information to herself. The less said about things he didn't know about, the better. And while she couldn't afford to go shopping for anything new at the moment, she'd dug out those fancy hunting clothes they'd bought together a few years before, and she looked and felt better than she had in a long time. She was making an effort, damn it! Only now her brother wasn't even around to appreciate her progress.

Pushing open the front door, she strode inside and went straight to the bar, nodding at Brandon as she did. He was the only one there on a Saturday night, and she tried not to think about what that meant for the future of her business. Right now she just wanted to relax and have a pint, and in her current foul mood she considered the lack of a crowd a blessing. Socializing with patrons had always been more Alice's forte. She never knew what to say to them.

She looked toward the fireplace and frowned. *Where's Maxine?* Dolly usually guarded the flock in the evening, freeing up the little border collie to lounge by the fire. The dog had become downright antisocial of late, but she couldn't usually resist the allure of a warm fire on a cold night. *If I have to walk down to Alice's grave tonight to retrieve you again, so help me, Maxine...*

The space behind the bar was empty and clattering sounds coming from the kitchen suggested that Maria was in the middle of something. Since interrupting Maria when she was in the middle of something was a recipe for disaster, Fiona walked around and proceeded to pour herself a pint. *Might as well help myself. That's the only good part of being the owner that I can think of.* She glanced back toward the fireplace and her breath caught at the sight of the strange woman sitting in the corner. She hadn't noticed her before, though looking at her, Fiona wasn't sure how that was possible.

Definitely not from around here, she thought as she took in the woman's thick, aubergine braids and chunky black glasses. She couldn't see all of her, but what was visible from behind the table was both shapely and trendily dressed. *London, maybe?* She finished pouring her pint, and when she looked back up, the woman stared right at her, nibbling her plump lower lip in a way that sent a shot of searing heat through her core. She nearly gasped at the powerful physical sensation. It had been a long time since she'd felt anything like it. With a shiver it dawned on her that the stranger's expression seemed to mirror her own. There was a hunger to it.

If ever there was a time to prove that she was ready to move on with her life, this would be it. Though she still missed Alice, she'd been alone for over a year now, and what were the chances that some undeniably hot and clearly interested woman would stroll through her sleepy little village any time soon? *And after all, I did promise Daniel to make a move on the next hot lesbian who wandered in, didn't I?* She choked back a laugh. Never in a million years had she expected to make good on *that* bet. On impulse, she grabbed a second glass and poured another pint of ale. Her hands shook with nervousness, but she steadied them as best she could and, taking one in each hand, carried the drinks to the woman's table.

"You looked like you could use a drink." She set the glasses down and pulled out the chair opposite the woman as casually as she could. "I haven't seen you in here before. Just passing through?" That's what she was hoping for—just passing through. Fiona wasn't looking for anything more than that. Fiona jumped in alarm as her foot connected with something warm underneath the table. There was a soft growl and she suddenly felt a complete fool as a familiar black and white head peeked reproachfully at her. "Maxine? Is that you?"

"Oh, do you know this little guy?"

"Girl, you mean," Fiona corrected, stifling a groan at the woman's accent. *American.* Of all the places in the world, why did the sexy stranger have to be from America? Given her brother's stunt, she wasn't feeling particularly charitable toward the place just now. "She's my dog, actually. I hope she wasn't bothering you. She's not usually this forward with strangers." *Unlike me. I hand out free drinks to every woman I meet because I'm just so very suave, can't you tell?* Fiona could feel the awkwardness building. She'd never guessed she'd grown this rusty at flirting.

"She's been a sweetheart, and great company." The woman's face brightened into a smile that nearly took Fiona's breath away. "Oh, bless your heart, you found something!" She'd said it not to Fiona, but in response to something or someone behind her.

Fiona turned to see Maria approaching with a plate of cheese and bread. The cook set it down on the table and cocked a curious eyebrow at Fiona, as if guessing what she was up to, but she didn't say a word. When Fiona turned back around, the woman was already shoving bits of cheese into her mouth as if she hadn't eaten in a week. Even in the midst of this gluttony, Fiona found her full lips unbelievably attractive. She took a long swig of her ale and tried not to stare.

"I'm so sorry. How rude of me!" After finishing a slice of bread and most of the cheese in a matter of seconds, the woman slowed long enough to give an embarrassed smile. "I've been traveling since last night and haven't had anything to eat. You wouldn't believe what it took to get here!"

"Don't let me stop you," Fiona replied with a wave of her hand. "So you've just got into town…er, I'm sorry, what was your name?"

"Paige." She stuck out her hand for Fiona to shake. "And yes, I just flew in today. At least, I think it was today. Did I mention I haven't slept, either?"

"I'm Fiona. Nice to meet you. So what on earth brings you to such an out of the way place like Holme? You look like more of a London girl, I'd think." *Now that had come out sounding somewhat flirtatious, right?* Fiona prayed she hadn't completely lost all skill.

"San Francisco, actually."

San Francisco? A most promising location. "Ah, that explains it. And you've come here for..."

"Rest and relaxation. And reflection, I suppose. The three 'r's. Apparently, in the past year since my girlfriend broke up with me, I've been sorely lacking in all three." She gave a self-deprecating shrug. "Or so I'm told."

"Oh, well I know how that is. I've recently been told something similar by certain individuals."

"Oh, is that right?" Paige arched one eyebrow. "Girlfriend broke up with you, too?"

Fiona stifled a laugh. *Trying to figure out if this is a friendly drink or if I'm hitting on you, are we?* Though Paige had been forthcoming enough on that front that Fiona figured she deserved a similar courtesy. "Close enough. She died."

"Oh my God," Paige gasped. "I'm so sorry!" She looked absolutely horrified.

Fiona covered her eyes with one hand, mortified. "No, no. I apologize. It was a lot less tragic-sounding when it was in my head. Obviously, I've got used to it. I didn't mean to—" Her voice trailed off, not sure what to say. *Great way to kill the mood!*

"How...how long has it been?"

Fiona took a breath. "Long enough that the people who say I need to learn how to move on probably have a point."

"I hear you on that." Paige lifted her glass. "To moving on?"

Fiona felt a tingle course through her as their eyes locked and she saw a flash of something that seemed to fill the evening with unexpected promise. She raised her glass and clinked the rim against Paige's. "To moving on."

Beneath the table, a warm paw scratched against Fiona's knees, accompanied by a whimper. "Excuse me a moment. It's time for Maxine to go out." She rose and opened the front door, shaking her head as the dog scampered up the hill toward the farmhouse. Such a predictable little thing. Fiona knew that Maxine would let herself in through the doggie door in the kitchen and be snuggled at the foot of the bed, softly snoring, by the time she got home. In fact, the only unexpected thing had been finding her curled up at a strange woman's feet. Not that Fiona could blame her. There was something about Paige that made her want to get close, too.

Fiona returned to the table and on impulse she skipped the chair and sat beside Paige on the bench instead. "So, where are you staying tonight?"

"Funny you should ask. There was a little mix-up

with my rental, so I guess I'm staying here, hopefully, at least until I can sort it out in the morning."

"Here? You mean in the pub?" Fiona felt a jolt as their knees bumped, which surprised her even more than what Paige had said. She'd left plenty of space between them when she sat, but somehow they'd drifted closer as they talked.

"Isn't it an inn? The sign said it was."

"No." Fiona knew she should elaborate, but she was too aware that their thighs had become sandwiched together, her right hand pressed so tightly in the crevice between them that she could feel the raised pattern of Paige's tights like Braille against her fingertips. "It used to be, only now it's…uh, not."

"Oh." Paige swallowed roughly and bit her lower lip. It might have been a look of disappointment, but then again, Fiona wasn't sure. Looks of disappointment weren't usually such a turn on to her. Although Paige's breathing had grown heavier, too, so perhaps the look was more of a response to the fact that her hand, which had become caught behind Fiona's back as they gravitated closer, had now slipped beneath the hem of Fiona's sweater and was tracing tiny circles against her bare flesh. Fiona was fairly certain her own thready pulse was directly linked to the latter, with absolutely no disappointment involved.

"You know, I—" Fiona stopped short, shocked to realize that she'd been about to invite Paige to come back to her house. *This is too absurd. We're complete strangers.* "I live just up the hill." Somehow the words tumbled out despite her attempt at restraint, as if Fiona were under a spell.

"You do?" Paige's fingers drew a line along the waistband of Fiona's trousers.

Fiona nodded, too scared to speak. *If you're going to start living again, you might as well start now.* She took a breath. "You could come back with me, if you'd like."

"You know, I think I might like that." Paige giggled, sounding as nervous as Fiona felt.

"Yeah? Good. I think I have some sandwich fixings I need help finishing."

Paige looked at the empty plate on the table, which was covered in crumbs of bread and cheese. She burst out in a hearty laugh and leaned so close that Fiona could feel her warm breath against her ear. "Well, there's an offer I can't pass up. Shall we?"

Body trembling, Fiona took Paige by the hand and led her out into the cold night.

"WELL, THIS IS IT."

Paige looked around with curiosity as Fiona found a place for her bag in the foyer. The house Fiona had led her to was a charming stone farmhouse, though a bit more bare inside than she'd expected. As they walked together into the living room, Paige was struck by the feeling of being in a house that wasn't quite a home, and she wondered how such an enticing woman had come to live in a place with so little personality. If this were *her* house, she knew exactly what she'd do to brighten it up.

There I go again, getting ahead of myself! If she was going to survive being single, she needed to learn to stop looking at the long-term relationship potential of every random hookup. Suddenly she felt too tongue-tied to say anything at all. *Random hookup? Ack! What was I thinking coming here?* She was attracted to Fiona without a doubt, but her impulsiveness terrified her. She'd never spent the night with a stranger before. This day couldn't become any more bizarre if it tried. Brittany would have a heart attack if she knew what Paige was up to. Or do a backflip. The fact that Paige wasn't sure which reaction was more likely was a big red flag that she would have to do her best to ignore if she didn't intend to turn tail and run this instant.

"So, you said something about a sandwich?" Paige giggled uneasily, knowing it was a stupid thing to say but hoping to break the tension.

"A sandwich?" Fiona's brow creased. "I can check. Though to be honest, that was more of a ploy to get you to come back with me."

"Oh really? Sandwiches are your secret weapon for picking up women?"

"I'm a bit out of practice, clearly." Fiona grinned, and the flutter it sent through Paige's belly reminded her exactly what she'd been thinking in coming here.

The smile faded from Fiona's lips, replaced with a look of concern. "I didn't mean to make it sound like you were obligated in any way. That is to say, I'm not trying to take advantage of your situation. I know you don't have a place to stay. I have a spare room. You're welcome to sleep there tonight if you don't want to—"

"I appreciate that." Now that Paige's nerves had settled, she really did *want to*. This was the sexiest woman she'd met in years and she'd question her sanity if she *didn't* want to. But it was sweet of Fiona to remind her she had the option to say no. "Just so we're clear, when you were offering to fix me a sandwich back at the pub, you really meant that you wanted to come back to your place and have wild sex with me. I did get that right, didn't I?"

"Yes." Fiona's cheeks flushed scarlet. "That's about right."

"Good. I just wanted to be certain. I'm a little out of practice, too. And just in case you were wondering, when I said that sounded like a nice idea, I wasn't really talking about having a sandwich, either."

"Well, it's good to know we're both singing from the same hymn sheet."

"The same hymn sheet?" Paige cocked her head to one side as she contemplated the unfamiliar expression. "Are you religious?"

"Not particularly, why?" Fiona gave her a wry look. "Haven't you ever heard that before?"

"No, never. And then I started thinking it was a

church thing, and if that was the case then maybe I shouldn't be tempting you with *sandwiches*, and—" Paige's words trailed off awkwardly.

"You seem nervous." Fiona's eyes were laughing but kind.

"This isn't something I usually do," Paige confessed. Thought it could have been embarrassing, her confession felt natural. In some ways, it was easier to be candid with this woman she'd just met than it ever had been with Veronica. "Like, ever."

"Me neither. Maybe I should put on some music to make us both feel more at ease?" Fiona could just be playing nice, but it was reassuring to know that she wasn't the only one being daring that evening.

"Yes, please." *Before we end up making some sandwiches and discussing theology and kill the mood completely*.

"Right, then. Music's in the bedroom. I'll just be a minute."

As Fiona started up the stairs to her room, Paige felt her limbs begin to tremble. *I'm going to ruin this, I just know it!* A small, rational part of her questioned whether that would be such a bad thing, but it was quickly beaten into submission by the swirling mass of hormones and lust that comprised the vast majority of her existence in this moment. *Of course it would be a bad thing!* She'd come to Yorkshire to get over Veronica and start living her life on her own terms again, and this was her chance to do exactly that.

She may not know Fiona well, but she liked what

she'd seen. They seemed to share a bond of loneliness that led Paige to believe that they really were 'singing from the same hymn sheet' as Fiona had said. She needed to take a risk eventually. Why not start where the stakes were low, just a night together with no expectations? What were the odds of meeting a gorgeous, funny woman who was interested in her on her very first night in town, anyway? *It's meant to be. There's was no other explanation.* Paige would be damned if she was going to allow her own insecurities and wishy-washiness to ruin it.

Filled with steely determination, Paige knew what she needed to do. In a flash, she unzipped her boots and kicked them into the corner, then stripped off her clothing into a pile next to them. Her pulse raced as she stopped, fingers trembling at the clasp of her bra. *Maybe this is far enough?* But she knew it wasn't. No, if this was going to happen without her chickening out, she needed to go all in. Bra and panties joined the heap, and she padded on bare feet up the stairs toward the bedroom. As she approached the door she heard a familiar jazz composition begin to play, a favorite from her performance repertoire, but usually a little too obscure for the typical jazz enthusiast. *It's a sign.* The song bolstered her confidence, and she struck a seductive pose against the door frame.

"Nice song." It took every ounce of her concentration not to break character. *Is this really me?*

Fiona jumped, her back to the door. "You startled

me!" She spun around and her mouth fell open when she caught site of Paige. "You're…uh…" Her eyes scanned up and down Paige's naked body, clearly at a loss for words.

Paige swallowed. "Trying to make certain we didn't have any other miscommunication about our intentions this evening."

"I'd say you're communicating quite clearly." Her gaze traveled slowly down Paige's body, halting at the small patch of chestnut curls between her legs. "Though I'll admit to feeling misled, as I see now that you're not a natural aubergine."

"Afraid not." Paige twirled the end of one braid around her finger, its amethyst highlights sparkling in the dim light. "And now you know *all* of my secrets."

Fiona took a step toward her, then another. "Somehow, I doubt that." Closing the distance between them, Fiona lifted a hand to either side of Paige's face and gently pulled her glasses away and set them safely to the side. Paige shivered when the rough wool of Fiona's sweater brushed against her taut nipples. She moved even closer. Her breath came in shallow gasps as Fiona's fingers slowly undid her braids and ruffled her hair until it hung in loose waves down her bare back. She felt Fiona's hands clasp behind her head, holding her steady as she leaned in for a kiss.

Heat coursed through her as Paige felt Fiona's lips meet hers, softly first, then more demanding. Their tongues touched, stoking an insatiable fire in her core.

Her teeth nipped at Fiona's lip, her breath catching as she felt one warm hand slide from her neck to cup her naked breast. Her hands fought against the tight waistband of Fiona's trousers, trying without success to gain access. She gave up in frustration, and settled for burying her fingers into fleshy buttocks, clasping them as tightly and deeply as the fabric would allow.

Fiona cried out in surprise, but evidently it was the good kind, because she pulled Paige firmly to her, pelvis rocking and grinding against Paige's bare thigh, her twill trousers deliciously rough against Paige's smooth skin. Paige gasped against Fiona's mouth as strong fingers pinched her nipple, sending shock waves coursing through her.

"You like that," Fiona murmured, shifting her hand to give attention to the other breast. She adjusted her touch in response to Paige's breathless moans until she'd got it just right, then slipped her free hand between Paige's legs, her fingers sliding through the wetness until at last they gained entry. At the first sensation of fullness, Paige was nearly sent over the edge.

How long had it been since someone had paid such close attention to what she wanted? Paige could hardly remember. It had been so long since she'd been with anyone but Veronica, who had never shown as much interest in Paige's needs as she had her own. But Paige didn't want to think about Veronica right now. She didn't want to think at all. All she wanted was to feel, to be filled with pleasure, and to give it in return. She slid her hands beneath the Fiona's sweater and lifted it over her head, tossing it to the floor. She needed to touch her, to feel their bodies come together. The bra quickly followed. Fiona's dark nipples beckoned, and it was her turn to experiment. Mirroring what Fiona had done, she grasped a pert nipple in each hand and was rewarded with a sharp intake of breath. "I guess you like that, too."

Paige grinned and took a step forward, backing Fiona against the edge of the bed. "So, what else do you like?" She plunged her head between plump breasts, breathing in her scent, searching for Fiona's nipple with her tongue.

When her tongue made contact. Fiona's knees buckled. They teetered for a moment, then Fiona lost her footing and tumbled out of Paige's arms and onto the mattress. With a hand on each of Fiona's thighs, Paige lowered herself to her knees on the floor. She slid her hands upward, grasping the waistband of Fiona's trousers. When she looked up, Fiona had propped herself up on her elbows and was gazing down at her, eyes dark with desire. Gaze locked, she tugged on the waistband, seeking to punish it for its prior lack of cooperation, anticipating the moment when the fabric would yield, when she could lose herself in the delicious excitement of exploration.

Paige trembled with the knowledge of how much she needed to be here right now, to experience the inevitable release that the evening promised. Though she didn't know her well, she felt that Fiona needed it just as much as her. She could see the same hungry look in her eyes, the same almost unbearable anticipation. Paige pulled a bit more, and overcoming their resistance, Fiona's trousers shifted and began to slide, revealing bare olive skin and a wispy bit of silk and lace that was all that stood between her and her goal.

The room went silent as a song ended, and Paige could hear her own heartbeat in her ears. She thought she might have heard Fiona's, too. She touched the tip of her tongue against her lips as she slid the lacy panties off and tossed them aside. Paige pressed her lips against Fiona's knee, dragged her tongue along the inside of her thigh, toward a tiny red birthmark in the shape of a strawberry. Paige tickled it with the tip of her tongue and laughter rang out like a bell. Fiona's legs opening wider for her as she approached the dark triangle of down between them. With her thumbs, Paige spread her open, her breathing so shallow that she had to shut her eyes to fend of lightheadedness. Eyes still closed, Paige moved her head closer, filling herself with the unfamiliar essence . Her tongue brushed against Fiona's center, making the woman cry out, and Paige kept still, savoring the newness of the moment. Then the soft strains of a new song hummed from the speakers, and their bodies moved in time with the music.

There would be no heartbreak or loss tonight. No

memories to haunt them. No promises for anything beyond this fleeting moment. They were two bodies together, discovering each other, but ultimately the lessons they needed to learn were for themselves alone.

SEVEN

FIONA STIRRED and stretched beneath the warm sheets. Beyond the window it was barely beginning to be light, though at this time of year the sun wasn't up until late. Regardless of the time, for once there was no rush to abandon the heavenly comfort of her bed because of the pleasure it contained, instead of the heartbreak. Turning on her side, she savored the feel of Paige's bare flesh against hers as she spooned her body around the sleeping form beside her.

She knew it was Paige without having to pause, without needing to open her eyes wider or spin through the narrative of the night before to piece together what had happened. She'd wondered if that would be the case upon awakening. It had been one of the many unknowns of sleeping with someone new. Would she mistake her for Alice, only to feel new cracks forming around her heart as the realization sank in? Would she feel regret? Those were the concerns that had plagued her the night before, at that moment when their eyes met and the music shifted, and she'd been certain there would be no turning back.

But her fears had been unfounded. She felt no confusion or regret. As for the experience itself, well... Fiona grinned into the darkness as she pulled Paige closer, nuzzling her lips against the back of her neck. As for *that*, there was really no reason it had to end just yet. It wasn't that she felt an emotional attachment. There had been an unspoken agreement between them that they'd spend the night together and nothing more. It was exactly what she wanted, and she'd have no trouble letting go when the time came. But on the other hand, neither of them had anywhere to be, and with a light drizzle of rain clouding the window, it was likely that the early morning grayness would last most of the day. Why bother getting out of bed so soon?

A warm lump near the foot of the bed stood to attention, and for the first time Fiona became aware of Maxine's presence in the room. She'd been unaccountably missing the night before, as if knowing the humans would want their privacy, but had appeared sometime in the night while they slept and curled herself up at Paige's feet. Once again Fiona wasn't sure what to make of her dog's attitude toward this woman who was now in her bed. Apparently, Maxine approved. But right now the dog was agitated, ears at attention and a growl emanating from her throat. She jumped off the bed and raced down the stairs, and Fiona knew she was heading for the doggie door. There were only two likely reasons for her behavior. Either Dolly had wandered into the yard and Maxine felt duty-bound to chase her off, or else someone was walking near the house.

A car door slammed outside and Fiona sat up at the sound, which seemed to be coming from her own driveway. *So it's option B, someone's coming to the house.* She frowned trying to puzzle out who it would be so early on a Sunday morning. Silently, so as not to wake Paige, Fiona slipped from the bed and threw on a robe, then tiptoed to look out the window. The sight of Jonas Clark, the vicar of the local church, walking along the path toward her front door did little to ease her confusion. *Is business so bad these days that the vicar's making house calls to round up the sinners?* He'd find it a hard sell at Fiona's door.

A loud tapping echoed up the stairway and Paige stirred. "What is that?" Her sleepy voice was low and gravelly, and reminded Fiona of all the reasons not to be out of bed.

"Nothing. Just the vicar knocking on the door."

Paige's eyes widened. "The who? I thought you said you weren't religious."

"I'm not! I have no idea what he wants. Probably to stop us from doing this." She leaned close and drew Paige's lips between her own, the heat between them flaring up in an instant. But the kiss ended in a groan as the tapping came again, more insistent this time. "Stay here. I'll go see what he wants."

The heavy door squeaked on its hinges. "Vicar?"

"Fiona! Good morning. I hope I didn't wake you."

Fiona shrugged noncommittally. "What can I help you with, Father Clark?"

"Now, Fiona. None of that formality. Just call me Jonas, remember?"

"Yes, of course." *Sorry, that's not going to happen.* She'd had a strict enough Roman Catholic upbringing in her youth to be convinced that it was a mortal sin to call a man of the cloth by his first name, even one of these liberal Church of England types like Father Clark. Though she no longer subscribed to much else that she'd been taught, that one just *felt* true, and she didn't see a reason to risk it. "So, you needed something?"

"Oh, yes! Margaret's come down with pneumonia."

"Margaret? Oh, you mean the church organist?"

"Yes, and it's terrible timing. We've a baptism today and it would be a shame to have no music."

At the mention of music, Fiona felt the familiar tightening in her gut. "Yes, well, you know I don't perform anymore. Besides, piano was never my strong point, and I've never so much as touched an organ."

"No, no. I know how you feel about your music, since Alice." There was a genuine sadness in his voice when he said her name. Unlike Fiona, Alice had been a somewhat regular member of the village's small congregation. "I would never ask you to go against that."

Fiona frowned, confused. "Then why exactly are you here, Father...Jonas?" That compromise on his name was as informal as it was going to get.

"Oh, I'm looking for your new tenant, of course!"

Just then a commotion of barking and growling interrupted and Fiona's head snapped around in time to see Maxine chasing Dolly on the far side of the garden. "Maxie! Stop that!" *Just what I need with those two. Wait, what did he just say?* "Sorry, my new what?"

"That American girl who's staying at your brother's cottage while he's away. She's supposed to be a bit of a musician. Plays the organ, from what Daniel said when I saw him at the pub the other night. She was supposed to arrive yesterday?"

Why am I always the last to find out? With a twinge of annoyance, it occurred to Fiona that every single person in the village might know more about her brother's business than she did. "I guess he forgot to mention it. Wait, hold on a moment," she added, remembering his note. She'd been so angry at him when she read it that she'd crumpled it and shoved it in her pocket when only halfway through. Her cape hung on a hook by the door and she pulled the ball of paper out now, smoothing it so she could read the rest.

Bullocks.

"Apparently I was supposed to leave my spare key

under the mat for this poor individual. Which I obviously did not. I'm sorry, Father, but I've no idea where this American organist of yours might be." A bumping noise came from the vicinity of her bedroom, and with it a sudden stroke of clarity. The mix-up with a holiday cottage. The American girl. *Now how do I explain to the vicar that I currently have his organist, naked, up in my bedroom?* She cringed as another loud bang reverberated down the stairwell, along with a decidedly female sounding grunt. *What is she doing up there?*

"Um, Fiona? There's a, um..." The vicar looked troubled, and she could only imagine what he must be thinking about this onslaught of strange noises coming from upstairs.

"Look, I think I can explain—" She paused as another volley or growls and barks drowned out her words. "Maxine! You leave that llama alone, or I *swear to God!*" She flinched at her unfortunate word choice and looked apologetically at the vicar, but his attention was elsewhere.

"Fiona, there's a, sort of an *aubergine*-haired woman wrapped in a sheet climbing out your upstairs window."

"What?" Fiona shot out the front door, past the vicar, to get a closer look. Her jaw went slack. Just beside her bedroom window was the ladder Fiona had used to tighten one of the shutters a few days before and forgotten to put away after. Balanced atop that ladder was Paige, her hair a wild technicolor cloud, her clothing a makeshift toga made of one of Fiona's bedsheets. One bare foot searched for a rung as the ladder wobbled. "Oh, God. Paige!"

More barking and growling came from behind the house, and then a tall white blur raced at full speed through the garden, followed by a snarling, yapping blur of black and white. They went careening into the ladder, knocking it several inches away from the wall, and then were off again in a flash of fur and teeth. Fiona's heart stopped as she watched the ladder sway. With a shrill scream, Paige went one way as the ladder went the other, and Fiona froze in horror as Paige tumbled to the ground. The sheet flapped from the ladder like a sail, while Paige lay splayed out on the grass beneath in all her glory.

"Cover your eyes, Jonas!" she hollered as she ran toward Paige. The fact that she'd used his first name hardly mattered now. There was little question she was hell-bound after this.

"My God, Paige, are you okay?" Fiona knelt beside her, breathless. She let out a sigh of relief as Paige moaned and blinked her eyes. At least she was conscious.

"What was that?"

"Maxine, chasing Dolly."

"Dolly? That wasn't another dog, was it?" Paige squeezed her eyes shut and moaned softly. "It happened so fast, but I could've sworn that was too big to be a dog."

"Dolly's a llama."

"Oh God!" Paige started laughing so hard that Fiona was afraid she'd lost her mind. "No, really? You named your llama Dolly?" She giggled some more. "Dolly llama?"

Fiona chuckled at the old joke. "That was my brother's doing. And speaking of my brother, this entire thing is all his fault, it would seem."

"It's his fault I got knocked off a ladder by a speeding llama?" Paige giggled again and this time it occurred to Fiona to worry about just how hard her head had hit the ground. They were going to need a doctor.

"I think you were meant to be staying at his cottage." Fiona straightened up and retrieved the sheet from the ladder, then draped it over Paige's naked frame—but not before sneaking another appreciative peek. "Only I didn't know you were coming, so I didn't put out the key."

Paige cocked an eyebrow. "So *that's* how I ended up in your bed last night."

"I'm so sorry." The comment may have been in jest, but Fiona's apology was sincere.

"Sorry I spent the night?" Her face grew serious.

"No, not sorry about that." Fiona grinned. "You know, I'd been looking forward to the sight of you all tangled up in my sheets again. I just hadn't imagined it would be in my garden."

Paige bit her lip sheepishly and giggled some more, until her laughter turned to a grimace of pain.

"We need to get you to hospital. Here, can you sit up, do you think?" Fiona slid her hand behind Paige's shoulder and gave her a gentle upward nudge. As Paige sat upright, the sheet slipped away. Without a thought, Fiona covered the exposed breast with her hand and a surge of heat went through her, despite the circumstances. It was clear from Paige's flushed cheeks that she'd felt it too.

"Are you ladies okay over there?"

Father Clark's voice caught Fiona up short. In her concern over Paige, she'd forgotten he was there. "Yes, we're fine." She straightened Paige's sheet as she spoke, wrapping it tightly around her and tucking in the end. Tempting as it was, it would hardly do to continue fondling her new lover's breasts in front of the vicar. "Don't you have a church to lead, Father?"

"Yes, well if you're sure you're alright..." He sprinted the several yards to his car, little more than a black blur with a white collar, and Fiona stifled a laugh. At least he looked as embarrassed over the whole situation as she was.

"Shall we try standing?" Fiona's brow creased in concern as Paige struggled to her feet with a cry of pain. "Where does it hurt?"

"My right ankle." Tears glistened in her eyes.

Fiona examined the ankle grimly. "It's already

bright red and swollen. You definitely need to see a doctor. Come on, I'll help you to the car."

"Um. Maybe I could get some clothes on first?"

Despite her worry, Fiona couldn't help but laugh. "I'm so sorry! I'd forgotten." She put an arm around Paige's body to support her weight. "What were you thinking anyway, sneaking out of the house without your clothes?"

"I don't know. I panicked!" Paige hung her head in embarrassment as she limped along. "I was raised Lutheran, you know, and not the fun kind. Missouri Synod, if that means anything to you. When I realized there was a minister at the door, I guess I lost my mind. Why was he here?"

"For you, actually. He was in need of a church organist this morning, and he seemed to think you could help. I didn't realize I should be asking if *you* were the religious one." They stopped beside the discarded pile of clothing in the living room. Fiona debated whether to watch as Paige unwound the sheet, but decided to politely look away. There was a much better chance they'd actually make it to hospital if she did.

"I'm really not, but I do know how to play the organ a little. I play at a wedding chapel run by an Elvis impersonator."

"How American sounding." She wasn't sure what else to say.

"Isn't it? It's a long story how I ended up there.

You wouldn't want to hear it. Okay, I'm ready. You can turn around now."

Fiona turned and studied Paige with a sense of wonder, this stranger who had walked into her life and caused equal parts pleasure and havoc in a matter of hours. Their acquaintance was meant to be fleeting, a convenient way for them both to meet a physical need. But here she was playing nursemaid to the woman, and faced with several weeks as landlord and tenant, besides. It was an unexpected turn of events, to say the least. And even more surprising, Fiona found that she very much wanted to hear exactly how Paige had ended up playing the organ for a fake Elvis. In fact, she couldn't imagine a better way to spend the day. It wasn't emotional attachment. Not yet. But it felt dangerously close, and that was the part she found most troubling.

EIGHT

"HEY THERE, GIRL," Paige cooed, balancing her weight on her crutches and dragging along her injured foot as she inched toward the garden wall. Just to the other side stood Dolly, her snowy-white face peering curiously at Paige. "I hear your name's Dolly. I'm Paige. It's about time we were properly introduced, don't you think? Considering you're to blame for this." She tried to wiggle her leg but it was immobilized in a giant plastic boot. Dolly showed off her mouthful of crooked teeth in a lopsided grin.

Allowing one crutch to drop, Paige reached out her freed hand and ran it through the soft fuzz on Dolly's head. She scanned the rolling field beyond the wall and found it devoid of life, the grass faded to a golden brown with winter's approach. It shone in the late morning sun like faded bronze. "So where are your sheep today, Miss Dolly? Is it Maxine's turn to guard them?"

Dolly reared up her head, exposing her teeth once more, and Paige could almost have been convinced that it was in response to hearing the border collie's name. Paige laughed and patted the animal's neck gently. "Oh, I see. Things are complicated between you and Maxine, are they?" At the edge of the field, two figures came into view that could only be Fiona and her dog. She gave Dolly a wry grin. "No, you're right. I have no idea what *that* would be like. I *never* find myself in complicated relationships with women."

It was one thing to allow travel-induced madness to temporarily suspend good decision making. A one-night stand was forgivable under the circumstances. One could argue it was almost obligatory. Likewise, freaking out about it after waking up in a stranger's bed the next morning was perfectly understandable. The part that Paige couldn't explain away so easily was why she'd thought wrapping herself in a sheet and sneaking out a second-story window in a foreign country had been a good idea.

Where did I think I was going to go? She'd been naked for heaven's sake, barefoot, and with all of her belongings sitting in a suitcase in Fiona's front hall. Even before she'd discovered that her no-strings-attached lover was also her new landlord for the next several weeks, that fact alone should have led her to pause long enough to come up with a better plan. One that involved having a passport. And pants.

The arrival of the minister had shaken her, but it wasn't the real reason she'd panicked. Paige had lied about that. No, what had spooked her so badly was the dream she'd had just before waking. Not a naughty dream. That would have made sense given the circumstances. The dream she'd had involved paint samples and fabric swatches. In her dream, she'd been deciding how to redecorate Fiona's sparse living room. And that could only mean one thing.

I am pathologically incapable of a one-night stand.

Though it pained her to admit it, Veronica had been right. As much as she tried to claim otherwise, she always had one eye firmly fixed on the next step. That hope was always there inside her, shimmering just beneath the surface, that *forever* was somehow a treasure just waiting to be scooped up and made hers. *Forever*. She'd done it with Veronica for years, so convinced that they were meant to be together that she ignored every sign that they weren't. She couldn't do it again.

Across the field, the figures of Fiona and Maxine had grown taller with their approach. They were close enough for Paige to see that Fiona once again wore a pair of skintight breeches that outlined every curve from waist to knee. She felt a shot of heat directly in her groin, which proved her point completely. It was a physical response, not an emotional one. Fiona was an attractive woman whom she'd known for less than forty-eight hours. They'd shared one amazing night together, but nothing about the situation suggested it was time to start picking out curtains, no matter what her dreams tried to say.

Temporary. Paige wondered what the dictionary definition of that word would be. *A state in which you are on vacation for a few weeks in a foreign country, where you have no friends, no family, and no job. See also the status of any relationship undertaken while in this state.* That basically covered it as far as Paige was concerned. Temporary, the opposite of forever.

Fiona was close enough now to make eye contact, but it was Maxine who made the first move. Racing away from Fiona and skirting along the edge of the stone barrier, the dog alternated between happy tongue-lolls directed toward Paige, and dagger-eyes-of-death aimed at her nemesis, Dolly. With a triumphant yip, she scooted under the gate and came to rest at Paige's feet. The way she stared up at Dolly with her tongue hanging out of her mouth felt deliberately taunting.

"Good morning, Fiona. Did you have a good sleep?" Paige hoped that her words conveyed how totally at ease she was with their new living situation, rather than implying that she was unnaturally focused on how Fiona might have spent her night. Or what she'd been wearing while doing it.

"How's your ankle?" Fiona looked at the discarded

crutch on the ground and frowned. "A sprained ankle and concussion are nothing to mess around with, you know. Dr. Ross said to take it easy for the next week."

"*Mild* concussion," Paige corrected. "And I have been. It's just that I heard a sound out here and wanted to see what it was. Turns out it was a llama."

"A very bad llama, who spent her night kicking down fences instead of guarding the sheep. They all got out again, and I've been up since before dawn rounding them up."

"You're the one who needs rest," Paige said sympathetically. "Especially after staying with me all day at the hospital yesterday."

Fiona nodded, clearly unable to argue the point. Passing through the gate, she bent to retrieve the fallen crutch and handed it to Paige. "Let's get you inside."

Once inside the cottage, Fiona helped Paige onto the couch, propping her injured leg onto the ottoman and setting her crutches nearby. "I'll just go put the kettle on," she said as she disappeared into the kitchen, reemerging a few minutes later with two large mugs of tea. "I put in the milk and sugar without thinking to ask. If that's not how you like it, I'll make a new cup."

"No, that's fine," Paige said, reaching for the mug out of a polite sense of duty. As far as she knew, there was nothing in existence that could be added to it to improve the taste of tea, but she could hardly say that to Fiona when she'd gone to the effort of making it. Besides, it felt so nice to have someone taking care of her that she didn't want to ruin it. "Thank you for all of your help yesterday and today. I still feel so ridiculous for what I did, climbing out that window."

"Well, it was just as much Dolly's fault as yours."

"Yes, I had a talk with her about that this morning."

Fiona lowered herself onto the couch beside her. "Now, when you say you had a conversation with her, do you think she talked back?"

"I didn't hit my head that hard, I don't think. Although she did express remorse over knocking over the ladder. I'm almost sure of it."

"Sounds like it's time for your pain medicine. You're delirious." Fiona fetched the bottle from the counter and handed two to Paige as she settled back down on the couch.

Paige looked from the pills in her hand to the mug of tea, which was the only form of liquid available to help her swallow them. She could ask Fiona for something else, but then she'd have to confess her disdain for drinking hot water with bitter leaves in it, and that could be awkward. Suppressing a groan, she popped the pills in her mouth and took a big swig. *That's actually not so bad,* she thought as the sweetened liquid tickled her taste buds. Whether the quality of the tea was simply better in England, or the milk and sugar had been added in just the right way, she wasn't certain, but she took a second sip and was shocked to find the taste was growing on her. *It's no dark roast extra wet latte, but...*

"You're quite the nursemaid, Fiona. I don't know what I would do without you." Paige held her breath, suddenly worried how Fiona would respond, but the woman just smiled shyly.

"Thanks. Well, I guess I got used to the medical routine with Alice."

"Alice?" Paige inhaled sharply as she made the connection. "Oh, was she your girlfriend? The one who—" Fiona nodded and Paige felt a pang of sympathy for her. "Do you mind if I ask what happened?"

"Cancer." Fiona shrugged. "Very aggressive, fast-moving. She'd barely found out she had it before she basically slipped away."

Paige was silent, trying to imagine how awful it must have been for her. "I'm sure she appreciated you taking care of her." She suspected it wasn't an adequate enough thing to say, but she could think of nothing else. Not wanting to end the conversation on such a somber note, and also suddenly aware of not wanting Fiona to leave, she attempted to change the subject. "Would you like to stay and watch a movie with me?"

Fiona lifted one eyebrow, as if uncertain what to make of the offer. Paige wasn't sure what she meant by it, either, except that she was enjoying this companionable time with Fiona more than anything she had in a long time, and she didn't want it to end. Finally, Fiona nodded and went to switch on the television. She chose a screwball comedy with not too much romance in it, and sat back down beside Paige, but not so close that any parts of them could touch. Paige could feel the deliberateness in her actions.

As the pain meds took effect, Paige felt her eyelids grow heavier and her attention waver. Somehow she drifted from her spot on the couch to being curled up with her head in Fiona's lap, but she was too sleepy to figure out how it happened or rectify the situation. Instead, she watched the movie through half-closed eyes and enjoyed the feel of Fiona's fingers absently stroking her hair. In some ways, this light touch was even more satisfying than the passion they'd shared before. There was more heart, more caring, in these caresses. Even in her semi-comatose state, Paige acknowledged that this could prove to be a problem, but one for another day.

They may have stayed like that for hours, Paige wasn't sure. She would have been just as happy to never move from the spot. As she drifted in and out, a soft humming surrounded her, a lullaby so sweet that if she'd been able to open her eyes, she was convinced she'd see an angel in the room. She was nearly asleep when she felt Fiona's body shift, the warmth of her replaced by a cool pillow beneath her cheek. A blanket was placed over her, and she felt gentle fingers tuck it close all around.

"Maxie, you stay here with Paige, okay?"

Paige heard a whimper in response, and the sound of a tail thudding against the living room rug, where the dog had curled up to join them at some point during the day. Then the front door creaked and she was alone in the cottage. The press of Fiona's lips against her temple before she left was certainly just a product of her imagination. There'd be no reason for Fiona to kiss her like that. Except that if it were just her imagination, why did she continue to feel the very real sensation of the moisture that Fiona's lips had left behind slowly drying on her skin?

PLINK. Plink. Plunk.

Paige's fingers idled on the piano keyboard as the notes faded away. *Thirty thousand dollars in student loans for a music degree and I've been playing the same three notes for the last hour.* She spun around on the stool and looked at the frozen movie image on her laptop. Maybe if she watched the scene one more time something would finally inspire her?

"Mike's going to kill me." She said the words out loud and Maxine, who was napping in the middle of the rug, pricked up her ears in response. "I've been working on this for almost a week and I'm getting absolutely nowhere."

Maxine stood and stretched, then padded across the room to rub her head against Paige's legs. Paige sucked in her breath as the dog's movements jarred her swollen ankle. She knew she should take another pain pill and put the big plastic boot that Dr. Ross had given her back on, but then she might as well give up on the idea of working for the rest of the afternoon. The pain pills made her brain feel fuzzy, and the clunky walking boot made it impossible to operate the piano's pedals while she played. Not that she should be moving her foot that way, but she was willing to suffer for her art if inspiration struck.

She scratched Maxine behind the ears and felt a surge of gratitude for the little dog's companionship. Ever since Fiona had let Maxine stay with her the first night, the border collie had taken up permanent residence in the middle of the living room floor by day, and at the foot of her bed by night. "You're a good girl, Maxie. Did you know that? Yes, you are!" Thump, thump went her tail against the floor in response. That Paige would have preferred the company of Maxie's owner in her bed at night was hardly the pup's fault, nor was the fact that aside from a once-daily visit to check on her well-being, Fiona had mostly been keeping her distance since watching movies with her that first day back from the hospital.

It was a ticklish situation, this thing between Fiona

and her. They'd entered into it with the silent understanding that it was a one night deal, nothing more than blowing off steam. And it had been steamy, alright. Explosive. Since neither one of them had expected to see the other again once it was over, they'd enjoyed a complete lack of all the usual inhibitions during their night together. Honestly, it had been the best sex Paige had ever had.

Only now they were stuck in close proximity to one another for the next eight weeks, and the inhibitions seemed to have sprung up full-blown in seconds. The attraction was still there too, but buried under a whole new layer of complications they hadn't counted on or wanted. Fiona had been looking in on her daily, even bringing her groceries or food from the Black Fleece, but since their unexpected closeness after the hospital, she'd made sure to leave the cottage well before anything had the chance to get remotely personal. Paige knew it was for the best, but it did still sting.

Paige shut the lid of her computer with a *snap*. Her head swam with exhaustion and confusion and more than a little longing, and she needed a break. "Come on, Maxie, you want a treat?" The dog's tail thumped even harder against the floor boards. "Okay, let's go!" She eased herself onto her good leg and took a couple of hobbling steps toward the box of treats on the mantle. She knew she should be using her crutches, but she'd left them clear on the other side of the room. *Just a few more steps.*

"What do you think you're doing?" Fiona's voice boomed from the front door of the cottage.

Paige spun around, a guilty expression on her face, as she grabbed the mantle for support. "I was just getting Maxine a treat." She tossed a biscuit to the dog, who gulped it down greedily.

"Where's your boot? And your crutches?" Concern tinged with exasperation colored her words as Fiona crossed the room and slipped her arm around Paige. Her body was warm and inviting, and Paige wished she could melt into it as Fiona helped her to the couch. "You're supposed to stay off that foot and keep it elevated," she scolded as she propped Paige's right leg up on the ottoman. With a gentle touch, she rolled up the hem of Paige's trousers and examined the injured ankle. "It's looking a little better today." She cupped Paige's heel beneath one hand and massaged her ankle lightly with the other. "How does that feel?"

It felt heavenly—not the ankle itself which still throbbed angrily—but the feel of Fiona's fingers on her skin as they inched their way higher up her leg. Before she could stop herself, Paige let out a little moan. Fiona looked up from where she knelt between Paige's legs and when their eyes locked, the sense of *déjà vu* sent a tingling through her core. Of course, last time their positions had been reversed, with Paige the one looking up from between Fiona's legs, her hands clenched on either side of Fiona's waistband, breathlessly anticipating the moment when the fabric would slip to reveal bare skin. From the spark in her eyes, Fiona was remembering it, too.

They hovered for a moment in that strange space between two equally plausible realities. One led to a friendly pat on the head and best wishes for a continued speedy recovery, the other to Fiona's teeth clenched around the lacy edge of Paige's panties as they slid down her legs toward the floor. Was it any wonder their interactions had become so difficult to navigate?

"I ran into the vicar today, down at the Black Fleece," Fiona commented, killing the mood in the most effective way imaginable. If she lived to be a hundred, Paige would never forget the searing humiliation of finding herself naked and spread eagle on the ground in front of the village priest. "He says the organist is still sick."

"Oh, that's a shame."

Fiona rolled Paige's trouser leg back down, then stood to fetch the plastic boot. "Apparently tomorrow's the start of Advent, and he's very distressed to still be without music."

"I could do it." Despite her desire to avoid the vicar and the bad memories he represented, the idea of getting out of the house after a week of sitting idle filled her with excitement. "I mean, if it's nothing too complicated." Aside from endless repetition of the Bridal March, church music wasn't exactly her area of expertise.

"I imagine he'd be grateful for whatever he could get at this point. But are you certain?" Fiona regarded her sternly as she fastened the strap on the walking boot. "You're supposed to be resting."

"Fiona, I'm so bored," Paige whined. She'd meant for it to sound more teasing than it did. It came out borderline pitiful. Something about the admission unleashed a swell of sadness inside, and she could feel tears stinging her eyes. "This isn't how I thought this trip was going to be. I was supposed to be strong and stand on my own. I didn't think I'd be like this."

"I'm sorry. I should have come by more this week. It's just that it's—"

"Confusing?" Paige shrugged. "It's not your fault. And you were kind enough to loan me your dog."

"Maxie? I doubt I could've kept her away if I tried. She likes you. But then, I like you, too. So I shouldn't have just left you here all alone in your condition."

"You like me, huh?" Paige chewed on her bottom lip as she giddiness tickled her insides.

Fiona nodded. "Of course I do. I mean, obviously I must or I wouldn't have asked you back to my place that first night. But I'll confess that it's more than that. I've come to enjoy your company. Honestly? I've been afraid I'd grow too used to you being here and it would make it harder when you leave."

"Me too! But I also didn't count on how hard it would be to be away from home for so long without a friend." Paige hesitated, gathering up her courage. "I know it's not what we'd planned, but I think we could try to be friends, don't you?"

Fiona let out a breath. "You know what? I do. And I think you could get out of the house long enough to play the music for the church tomorrow, too. But only if you promise to follow Dr. Ross's orders. You're wearing the boot the whole time, and bringing the crutches with you, too. I can drive you there in the morning and pick you up after the services."

"Really? You would do that for me?" Paige's face lit up in a grin. "Thank you!"

"What are friends for?" Fiona gave Paige's knee a friendly pat. "Besides, it will get me on the vicar's good side, and considering recent circumstances, I don't see how that could hurt."

NINE

THIS IS nothing like the organ at the Velvet Elvis. Paige surveyed the massive pipe organ with growing trepidation. She'd never expected a little village church to have an instrument like this. The entire wall was covered with gleaming pipes, with a console consisting of six keyboards, hundreds of stop-knobs, and a full pedalboard below the bench. She'd learned on one like it in college, but the one she used for weddings was more of a glorified electric keyboard with a few extra knobs and switches. But this type of thing was probably like riding a bicycle, right? She inhaled deeply. *I can do this.*

"Can I get you anything, Miss Ridley?" The vicar approached Paige at the organ, his eyes trained nervously on the tips of his shoes which were poking out from beneath his robes.

"I think I'm all set," she responded, turning to

smile at a spot right around his elbow. It was a system they'd hashed out quickly between them, that seemed to work for them both. *As long as we never make direct eye contact, neither of us ever has to acknowledge the unfortunate incident of the Ladder and the Lost Sheet.* "The hymns themselves are familiar to me, and as for the arrangements, I'll keep it simple, if that's okay with you."

"Yes, that's fine. I'll just go join the others, and you can start the processional music when the doors open."

"Uh huh," she mumbled, this time busying herself with straightening the sheet music so she wouldn't need to look at the vicar's face.

She shifted uncomfortably on the bench, glaring at the walking boot that weighed down her foot. It was tempting to take it off. This type of organ was designed to be played with both hands and feet simultaneously; an impossible feat with a huge chunk of plastic strapped to you. But she'd promised Fiona to keep it on as a condition of coming here today, and she wasn't about to go back on her word. She could play well enough with just her hands, and keep her feet out of it.

As she struck the first chord, Paige nearly laughed out loud. She'd forgotten how loud a real pipe organ could be! But it was fun, too, and the professional musician portion of her was thrilled with the chance to play on such a beautiful, old instrument. Even the pageantry of the traditional procession, with the richly embroidered vestments and pungent incense, left Paige suitably impressed. Which is why it seemed so strange, as the final notes echoed through the church, to hear snickering coming from the congregation. Followed by a familiar bark.

Eyes wide, Paige turned from the console to see Maxine trotting up the center aisle, just a few feet behind the vicar who was bringing up the rear of the procession. To her credit, she had a reverent expression on her canine face that Paige doubted few dogs could surpass, but she also doubted that Father Clark would see it that way. Her fear was confirmed a few seconds later when Maxine answered the priest's chanting of the opening greeting with a mighty howl, a miserable noise that sounded almost exactly like the priest if she were being honest about it, and the congregation dissolved into a fit of laughter.

"Maxine!" She hissed in the loudest whisper she could manage. "Bad dog! Come here and sit!"

Unrepentant, Maxie bounced her way up to the organ and settled in beside it with an immensely self-satisfied look. Paige silently cursed her luck. She'd known that Maxie was unhappy about being left behind at the cottage that morning, but it had never occurred to her that she would follow Fiona and her all the way to the church. Under any other circumstances, she would have been touched by her loyalty, but as it was, having already turned a thousand shades of scarlet, Paige spent the rest of the service glaring at the dog and trying not to melt into a puddle of embarrassment on the church's ancient flagstone floor.

There were only two hymns that day, classic Christmas songs that Paige had learned decades ago, during her piano lessons when she was just a kid. She got through them smoothly, and Maxine managed to sit quietly without joining in. By the time the final song came along, Paige's muscle memory for operating the complicated organ had returned, and she felt inspired to add some extra flourishes as she played. There was really nothing quite as exhilarating as playing for an audience, after all.

The congregation loved it, and soon they were singing along in full voice, the pipes belting out the festive holiday tune. Paige was completely caught up in the music. It was the type of moment every musician dreams of, when everything comes together in perfect harmony. Her audience was happy, and she was happy, and pretty soon she felt surrounded by an overpowering sense of joy. So much so that her feet began dancing along the pedalboard to *really* get things rocking.

Which turned out to be a huge mistake.

She didn't know it at the time, but the spacing of the pedals on the pedalboard and the width of the plastic walking boot on her injured foot were nearly identical. Which meant that when she got caught up in the moment and forgot about her unusually clunky footwear, the boot slipped between two of the pedals and became lodged. Sweat broke out on her brow as she realized that she was trapped. Like a pair of Chinese handcuffs, the harder she pulled, the more stuck she got. Some quick thinking on the keyboard covered the problem for a moment, but there are only so many times you can dramatically end a familiar piece of music before the congregation expects it to actually end. With her foot still stuck and the pipes still blasting, Paige's panic reached epic levels.

Which is when Maxine decided to come to the rescue.

The little dog, sensing Paige's distress, leaped onto the pedalboard, landing with a crescendoing cacophony of sound. She tugged at Paige's trouser leg and ran in circles and barked, and finally she flung herself with all her might at Paige's torso. Paige's foot pulled free and she toppled backward, and she and Maxine both landed with a thud on the opposite side of the bench. Paige was flat on her back against the icy flagstones, and Maxine was pressed against her nose and mouth, cutting off her dwindling air supply. By this time, the quick-thinking vicar, possibly because he was already aware of Paige's talent for mischief, had begun to usher the congregation out the door. However, most of them were still well within range to hear Paige's voice when she screeched, "Jesus Christ, Maxine! Get your smelly ass off of my face!"

It was a start to the Advent season that would not

be forgotten in the Holme Valley for many years to come.

With the service ended in spectacular fashion, Paige pressed herself into a space between the wall and the organ console, and prayed to disappear. She was shaking and fighting back tears when the sound of footsteps echoed through the empty church. She wiped her eyes and stood to see a man approaching. He had the rough and ruddy look of a farmer, and his smile was kind as he caught her eye.

"Miss Ridley?"

"I'm afraid so."

He put out his hand. "Pleased to meet you. I'm Liam Hart. I understand that you're staying at the Hart —er, that is to say the *Blake* farm. My cousin, Alice, was Fiona's—"

"Oh, yes, of course!" At the mention of Alice's name, Paige's head cleared. *Alice, the girlfriend who died. Shit.* "I'm so sorry for your loss."

"Thank you. That's very kind. So, I hear you're a musician."

"Then you must not have been listening very closely during the service just now."

Liam chuckled. "It was an interesting morning, to say the least. But I heard from Daniel before he left that he was doing a house swap with an American musician, so I assume that's you?"

Paige nodded, perplexed. "Why, is someone in the village looking for music lessons?"

"Actually, my family is working with the church to organize the Christmas festival this year, as a fundraiser for the charity we've established in Alice's memory."

"Oh, how nice!" Paige's brow wrinkled, uncertain how she fit into any of this.

"We've included a special musical program, a concert before the Christmas Eve service, and we could really use the input of a professional just to see if we're on the right track. Jonas—the vicar, that is—suggested we talk to you."

Paige cocked an eyebrow. "The vicar? Recommended me?"

"Of course. Why wouldn't he?"

Indeed. Paige could think of several reasons, starting with the part where she was caught sneaking out of Liam's cousin's girlfriend's bedroom in the wee hours of the morning, naked as the day she was born, and ending with her screaming the Lord's name in vain at the top of her lungs just a few minutes prior in the very same room in which they were now standing. Paige shrugged. "No reason, I guess."

"The thing is, we want to do this right. We have some ideas already, of course, but do you think you could help us put the finishing touches on it?"

Paige considered. On the one hand, she'd never put together a musical program before. She didn't know the village, or what they were expecting. And she hadn't exactly made the best impression since her arrival. But on the other hand, her background made her qualified to do it, and she'd just been complaining about not having enough to do. Besides which, it was for Fiona's Alice.

She hadn't known Alice, of course, but Fiona had loved her and would certainly be involved with any charity in her girlfriend's name. And Paige valued their budding friendship and wanted to make sure they got off on the right foot, so to speak. What better way than to help organize a fundraiser? Finally, Paige nodded. "Okay. I'll give it a shot."

Liam grinned. "Fantastic!" He handed her an envelope he'd had tucked beneath his arm. "Here's some information about all of the activities that are planned. Officially the festival starts tonight with the Christmas parade in Holmfirth. The committee meets tomorrow to discuss the Christmas markets and the music program."

She took the packet from him and assured him she'd make it to the meeting and parade if she could. Her spirits now lifted after the terrible start to the day, Paige took her crutches and limped outside to the churchyard to look for Fiona. She smiled as she anticipated sharing the news about her role in the festival. It felt good to be getting involved in something that would show Fiona how grateful she was for the care she'd shown her in the past week.

FIONA STOOD beyond the churchyard gate, her head turned away from the stone memorials as she searched the sea of Sunday worshippers for Paige. She wasn't quick to emerge, and Fiona couldn't blame her. Despite her resolve not to get too emotionally invested in her new tenant, as a former musician herself, she couldn't help but feel curious to hear her play. She'd sneaked in toward the end of the service and witnessed the whole fiasco. *Poor Paige!* Maxine might find herself in a kennel for the next several weeks if she continued to wreak havoc like this.

Fiona felt a chill move through her as a familiar, ruddy face showed through the crowd. *Liam. What's he doing here?* She couldn't recall Alice's cousin being particularly religious last time she'd checked. He used to come to the Black Fleece on Saturday night to raise a ruckus, and be more likely to spend Sunday mornings in bed with a hangover than in a church pew. Of course, that was before Alice's death. Maybe that had changed him. Though she doubted it, it's not like she kept close enough tabs on the Hart family any more to really be certain.

Her eyes narrowed as she caught sight of Paige exiting the church just after Liam, stopping with a friendly smile as he held out his burly hand for a shake. *What could Liam want with Paige?* Uneasiness pricked her skin like an itchy sweater. There was just something about the man that she didn't trust. He was pleasant enough on the surface, but underneath she'd always suspected a nasty streak. She'd been certain, for example, that he'd put up Alice's headstone without consulting her out of spite, but without proof she'd eventually dismissed the thought. Seeing him with Paige brought all her misgivings about him racing back.

"Fiona!" Paige waved, then maneuvered her crutch back into place and made her way toward where Fiona stood. "There you are!"

"Hi, Paige! How was it?" Fiona asked, feigning ignorance.

"It was…a unique experience." Paige made a face while Fiona tried not to laugh. "I'd rather not relive it, though I think it's safe to say the vicar will think twice before asking me to play again. But I've just had the most exciting offer!"

"Is that so?" Fiona glanced suspiciously toward where Liam had stood, but found that he had gone. "Well, why don't we head over for Sunday roast at the Black Fleece, and you can tell me all about it? Maria makes an excellent roast."

"That sounds nice, but," Paige's expression grew pensive, "what about going into Holmfirth for a bite to eat before the Christmas parade, instead? My treat. Not a date or anything like that," she added hastily. "Just as a thank you since you've been taking such good care of me all week."

"Christmas parade?" Fiona's heart lurched. "Is that today?" Alice had made such a big deal over that stupid parade, and every year Fiona had found a reason to miss it, until last year when it had been too late.

"Alice's cousin, Liam, was telling me about it. And, well I might as well just tell you the news now. He's asked for my help in organizing a musical program as part of the festival to raise money for Alice's charity!" Paige beamed with excitement, but Fiona felt her insides go numb.

"I see." *So that's what Liam had wanted.* Her stomach tightened into a ball. Had he guessed at the connection between Paige and her before he sought her out, or was it just a coincidence?

Paige's brow furrowed. "Fiona, what's wrong? I thought you'd be happy. I was so glad to be able to help! It's not that you feel uncomfortable working together on this, is it?"

"I have nothing to do with that charity." Her words came out clipped.

"Oh." Fiona could see the questions in Paige's eyes. "I guess I just assumed."

"It's run by her cousins. We're not…" Her voice trailed off, not sure where to begin. "A *music* program, did you say?"

Paige nodded. "Yes. Did Alice like music?"

No, she resented the hell out of it every time it took me away from home. "I suppose. But, why did Liam ask *you?*" It seemed a fair question, considering that Fiona was a professional musician, not to mention Alice's partner, and no one had bothered to breathe a word of it to her until now.

"Oh, well I'm a musician," Paige replied.

Considering what she'd just witnessed in the church, Fiona raised an eyebrow at that assertion.

"Piano, mostly," Paige continued, seemingly oblivious to Fiona's skepticism. "I do some original compositions, too. I earned a music degree from San Francisco Conservatory."

"Oh!" Fiona considered this revelation with surprise. She'd had no idea they had that in common. She opened her mouth to say that she'd studied at the Guildhall School, but hesitated. That part of her life was over now. It seemed pointless to bring it up. "I hadn't realized."

"And I hadn't realized that you weren't involved in this fundraiser. It sounds like it might be a sore subject for you, and I'm afraid I've overstepped by getting involved. You're not mad at me, are you, for saying yes? I can still tell them no."

Paige's quick comfort meant a great deal. But it was Fiona's problem, not Paige's. She sighed. "No. Of course not. I'm sure your input will be a nice addition to the festival, and if you want to help out, you should."

"And you'll come with me to the Christmas parade?" Paige's eyes shone with excitement.

Fiona felt a pang of guilt as she recalled how many times Alice had said the same thing, only to be disappointed. "Yes. Let's go to the Christmas parade." If Paige wanted to see the parade, then they would see the parade. Even though this was strictly a friendship and she had every intention of keeping it that way, Fiona wasn't about to start repeating mistakes from the past with someone new.

TEN

"I HADN'T REALIZED this place would be so crowded," Fiona said, feeling glum. The new gastro pub in Holmfirth was bustling on a Sunday afternoon with more people than the Black Fleece had seen in months. A part of her had hoped the downturn in her own business was a reflection of a more widely spread phenomenon, but that clearly was not the case. "I guess plenty of people are still eating out these days, just not at the Black Fleece."

"I'm sure it's mostly because of the parade," Paige offered consolingly. She pointed to the corner of the pub. "I think I see a table over there."

As they settled in, Fiona took a look at the menu and frowned. "The prices are higher than the Black Fleece. Not as many choices, either."

"I just thought it would be fun to try someplace new." Paige said, looking apologetic.

"No, it's fine. To be honest, I'm feeling jealous. Business at the Black Fleece hasn't exactly been booming lately. I wish I knew what kind of magic this place had to be doing so well."

Paige tapped a finger against her lip thoughtfully. "Are you listed in the Christmas book?"

Fiona shook her head at the unfamiliar term. "What's that?"

"There was a copy in the packet that Liam gave me this morning. It's a book of shops and restaurants throughout the valley that are sponsoring the Christmas festival. Apparently it's providing a lot of publicity."

"In case you hadn't guessed, I wasn't exactly born doing this." Paige's brow knit in confusion, and Fiona continued. "Running a farm and pub aren't exactly in my blood." Fiona sighed. "And I'm afraid I'm not very good at either."

"So you weren't born here?"

"In Yorkshire? Goodness, no! Most people can tell just by looking at me or listening to my accent, but I'm forgetting that you're American so it may not be as obvious. No, I'm from London, by way of the British West Indies."

"British West Indies? Like, the Caribbean?"

Fiona nodded. "My dad's with the Diplomatic Service."

"He's an ambassador?" Paige asked, sounding impressed.

"Nothing quite so grand. He's just a mid-level civil servant. He met my mom on one of his assignments overseas. She's from Montserrat originally, of Irish and African descent like most of the people there. It was a completely normal background to have growing up, but around here the combination's a bit more exotic."

"Well, I think it's a very nice combination. I would never have guessed."

"Trust me, between my darker hair and skin tone, not to mention the way I speak, people in West Yorkshire usually peg me for an outsider right away."

Paige sat silently for a moment. "Has it caused problems for you?"

Fiona shrugged. "I mean, not in London. And when I moved here I was with Alice, and her family's been in the valley forever. So I felt like I fitted in, mostly. Now that she's gone, I'm not so certain." If business was booming at every establishment but hers, she had to consider the possibility that it had tapered off after Alice's death because the locals didn't think that she and her brother belonged.

"Maybe you need to find ways to get involved in the community. Show them you're here to stay. Like the festival committee, for example. There's a meeting tomorrow. You should come."

Coming from anyone else, Fiona's hackles would immediately have been raised and she would have resented the interference. But when Paige made the suggestion, it was like she'd handed Fiona a toasted crumpet, with just the right amount of butter on top. It was simply impossible to contemplate her doing such a thing with anything less than the best of intentions. So, Fiona was willing to consider that she might have a point. She'd kept to herself a lot the past year, too wrapped up in her own pain and guilt to pay much attention to anything around her. "Perhaps you're right. With that foot of yours, I should probably drive you there, anyway. Maybe I'll stay a bit, and see what it's about." Though Fiona appreciated Paige's optimism, she wasn't completely convinced going to a meeting would be enough. And there was Liam to consider. Still, it wouldn't hurt to give it a try.

Feeling her stomach rumble, Fiona pointed to the menu. "Do you know what you'd like? I'll go put in the order."

When the food arrived, Fiona's heart sank even lower than it had at seeing a room filled with diners. On her plate was the most elegant looking pub food she'd ever seen. "It's almost too pretty to eat."

"*Almost*. But I'm starving." Paige scooped up a forkful and put it into her mouth. Her face grew thoughtful as she chewed. "It's not bad. But it's not as good as Maria's. She's a very talented cook."

Fiona nodded in agreement. "She is. I have no idea how I'll manage once she has the baby."

"When is she due?"

"January." Fiona fought back a wave of panic as she mentally counted up the weeks. "Finding a cook to fill in for her is one thing, but Maria knows the business better than I do. She and her husband Brandon pretty much run the whole place." *With no help from me. Since Alice's death, I've been in a fog.* This hadn't bothered Fiona much before, but now that she was discussing details with Paige, her stomach sank with each admission.

"Is there anything I can do?"

Fiona felt a stirring in her heart at the kind offer. But as much as she wanted to accept, she knew she needed to put a stop to it. It would be too easy to grow dependent on Paige for help, like she had Daniel. More worrisome, too, was the risk of becoming too attached to the aubergine-haired optimist. "Don't you have a music festival to plan? If you keep volunteering to help with things around here, you won't have any time left to enjoy your holiday!"

"It's only partially a holiday, you know," Paige replied. "I'm supposed to be working on a score for a friend's film. Which is probably why I'm looking for a distraction."

"It's not going well?"

Paige made a face. "That's putting it mildly. Honestly, the past year since Veronica left, I've been in a fog. I've lost my inspiration and I'm not sure how to get it back. I keep thinking maybe this music festival will give me something to feel confident in, so I don't become completely convinced I'm a fraud." Paige nibbled on her lip, her eyes downcast. "I'm sorry. You must think I'm being a total drama queen. One of the hazards of having an artistic temperament, I guess."

Fiona nodded silently, not certain how else to respond. She knew exactly what Paige was going through. The loss of inspiration, the crippling self-doubt; she felt it, too. That and guilt had ended her career. *Is this why I've felt so drawn to Paige?* Fiona wondered if somehow she had sensed this common bond. But instead of raising her spirits, it made her more depressed. How else was she supposed to feel when the one person who might understand her was just a stranger passing through?

With dinner ended and the festival about to begin, Paige and Fiona made their way outside. It had grown dark while the women were inside the pub, and above them, suspended between the buildings up and down the road, white Christmas lights twinkled magically. The evening had turned raw, with a biting wind that whipped down the narrow main street. A sizable crowd had already begun to form, and well-bundled children lined the sidewalks in both directions, waving glow sticks and lanterns.

Paige let out a gasp and put her gloved hands to her cheeks. "This wind is like ice!"

Fiona assessed her friend's attire warily. Her wool coat and gloves seemed warm enough, but she lacked a hat or scarf. "You're going to freeze. Here." She unwrapped the long wool scarf from around her own neck and draped it over Paige's head. "Wrap this around your head and neck."

"What about you?"

"I'll be fine. I'm more used to the cold." Fiona pulled her tweed cap down tightly toward her ears and turned the collar of her coat up to cover her exposed skin. "I'd say we could walk over to the Christmas market and find some hot cocoa at one of the stalls, but between your foot and this cold, I'm not sure we should wander too far."

With a grateful smile, Paige wound the scarf around her as many times as she could. "How's this?"

Fiona burst out laughing. "You look like an aubergine-haired Russian grandmother. But in a good way."

Paige replied with a snort. "No offense to Yorkshire, but I'm really regretting not being somewhere a lot warmer right now."

"I couldn't agree more! Last year when I was in Sydney..." Her voice trailed off as she remembered why she'd been there, and what it had cost her. That part of her past wasn't something she was prepared to talk about with Paige. The first strains of a marching band playing Christmas carols reached their ears, and Fiona pointed down the road, thankful for the distraction. "Look, the parade's starting!"

As parades go, this was a small one, filled with local children and homemade costumes. Though she didn't know any of the participants, Paige seemed enchanted by it nonetheless, and the longer she watched, the more Fiona felt it, too. *Christmas*. Fiona would have sworn she didn't even like the holiday much. She'd never understood why Alice made such a big deal about it. But the longer she stood, steeping in the Christmas spirit that surrounded her, the more she could appreciate its appeal.

There was a magical quality to the celebration, from the flickering glow of lanterns and candles as the marchers passed by, to the familiar music played by the local school band. It was simple and charming. It promised all the comforts of family and home, and whether it could ultimately deliver or not, for a moment Fiona basked in the warmth of belonging. Her heart was bursting with affection for her adopted home, for her farm and the animals, the people around her in the streets. Even stronger than those were the emotions she felt for the beautiful woman who stood beside her, though she pushed that realization aside, unexamined, and pretended it was just more of the same holiday happiness that infused the night.

When the final float passed, featuring Santa in his sleigh, the spectators began to shift closer to the Christmas tree in the center of town. As people jostled and pushed their way past, Fiona eyed Paige's booted foot with concern. Paige had left her crutches in the car because of the crowds, and without them her pace was slower and her foot more vulnerable to a careless passerby. Reaching out, Fiona tucked her hand beneath

Paige's arm and pulled her aside, away from the throng of people.

"Let's watch from here," she suggested, pointing to a set of steps that offered a view of the square. "It'll be safer for your foot."

Paige nodded and took Fiona's hand as she helped her up the steps. Now that they were away from the crowd, the chill of the wind hit them full force. With a shiver, Fiona slid her arm around her companion's waist, turning her own body to block the wind while pulling her closer for warmth.

Paige nestled into her and turned her head, her expression tender. "Thank you." She didn't say why she was grateful. It could have been just for the hand up the stairs, or for blocking the wind. Or maybe it was for companionship on a beautiful evening, an evening that, unlike most, wasn't spent alone. At least, that was the reason Fiona's heart was filled with thankfulness in that moment. Thankfulness, and something else. Something that Fiona was afraid to admit was there, but was impossible to ignore; this sense that she'd found someone who understood her in a way that *no one* had before.

She realized with a start that she was staring, and Paige must have realized it at the same time because she let out a breathy laugh, but didn't look away. The pull of her smoky-gray eyes, partially hidden in the reflection of twinkling Christmas lights in her glasses, held Fiona captive. As she had that night in her bedroom, Fiona reached out and gently pushed the frames up until they were buried against the thick knitted wool of the scarf on Paige's head. Now the fairy lights sparkled in Paige's eyes instead, and still Paige continued to watch her, unblinking, while Fiona continued to cling to the notion that being just friends was still a viable option.

As they stood there, frozen in place, the lights on the giant village tree lit up. At the same moment as the lights switched on, tiny white flakes of snow began to fall, proving that even the curmudgeonly Yorkshire weather had fallen victim to the holiday magic that swirled around them. And if the weather couldn't hold out against it, how could Fiona hope to stand a chance? She tilted her head and closed her eyes, and pressed her mouth against Paige's lips.

Cheering echoed in her ears, and while she knew that it was probably the crowd reacting to the tree being switched on, Fiona couldn't entirely discount the possibility that it was the sound of her own emotions celebrating victory as they took over her brain. Kissing Paige was a reckless choice, but that didn't mean she planned to stop. Instead, as Paige moved to deepen the kiss, she went along without a second thought. She would regret it in her leisure if she had to, and blame the fairy lights and snow. But not until tomorrow.

ELEVEN

PAIGE'S EYES darted around the classroom at the village church as the vicar cleared his throat and called the meeting to order. *Still no Fiona.* Her car had been parked in the driveway this morning but she hadn't answered the door when Paige knocked. Paige had finally given up and driven herself to the committee meeting using the rickety old car Daniel had left for her. It had been a harrowing experience that she would do best not to think about too much if she ever planned to complete the return trip home. She'd thought Fiona was just running late and would show up before the meeting was called to order, but clearly she'd been mistaken. So which one was it? Had she chickened out on participating in the festival planning, or was she too embarrassed to face Paige after kissing her the night before?

They hadn't talked about it at the time, but what

had happened between them on the steps at the tree lighting had been the most natural thing in the world as far as Paige was concerned. There'd been a tree, and carols, and snow—*snow, for heaven's sake!* It had been like standing in the middle of a Christmas snow globe come to life. How could they *not* have kissed under those circumstances? Now *that* would have been unnatural. It didn't have to mean anything.

Of course, it didn't have to *not* mean anything, either. The more thought she gave it, the more Paige opened to that possibility, too. She had another several weeks in Yorkshire before she flew back home, and there was only so much introspection a person could take. Fiona provided a deliciously appealing distraction, not to mention a warm one. Paige had seriously underestimated how cold a winter in Yorkshire would be. Having an interesting companion to spend time with during the day and a cozy body to snuggle up with and enjoy during these endless nights wouldn't be the worst thing in the world. It didn't need to mean anything more than that.

A woman stood in front of the committee and started to deliver a financial report on the stall rentals for the Christmas market. Paige struggled to keep her tired head from bobbing. She hadn't slept well in her lonely bed the night before, where the memory of Fiona's lips against hers had replayed itself in her imagination well beyond a reasonable hour.

The subject matter of the meeting didn't help her

fatigue. According to the agenda, the music program wouldn't be discussed until halfway through. The rest of it had nothing to do with her, and even when they got to the part that did, she wasn't sure what she would be able to contribute. She'd made a few notes of suggestions that might help, but the real heavy lifting had already been done. Her notepad filled with intricate pencil doodles as the speakers droned on.

"And now we'll take a moment to introduce our newest member, Miss Ridley."

Paige's head snapped to attention at the sound of her name and she smiled shyly at the room of strangers who were all staring in her direction. "Hi!"

"Miss Ridley is a musician from America who is going to help us with the Christmas Eve concert to raise funds for our beloved cousin Alice's charity," added Liam, who sat at the front of the room. There was a polite murmuring of approval at his words. "Miss Ridley, did you have any suggestions to share with us?"

"Um, yes, just a few." She shuffled through her notes with one hand as she adjusted her glasses along the bridge of her nose with the other. "So, mostly I'd say you've done a very nice job putting together the program. The choices of music are solid, and offering both choral and instrumental pieces should please a large crowd. Really my only suggestion would be to add a bigger name performer to headline the evening, but I know there's not—"

"See! That's exactly what I've been telling you all," interjected a portly man with red hair and a thick mustache who waggled his finger at Liam as he spoke.

"Now, Harry," the vicar implored, "you know the rules! If you could just raise your hand—"

"That's alright, Jonas," Liam responded. "Harry makes a good point. This is an issue he's raised before."

"Darn right it is! I've been saying for months that if we'd just asked her—"

"Harry," Liam said soothingly, "you know she wouldn't do it. There was no point in asking."

Harry harrumphed, an action that made his pink chin disappear into the folds of his neck. "Someone else, then. Tickets are selling well enough to the locals, but we'll need to draw a larger crowd for this to be a success. If people are going to travel all the way into the valley for a concert, they want a big name. It's like the American girl just said!"

Paige's eyes widened at the reference to herself. With the sudden tension in the room, she felt like she'd gone out for a quiet stroll and wandered into the middle of a battlefield by mistake.

There was another murmur from the crowd. "That's true," one woman added. "The boys' choir from York is nice and all, but for the price of the ticket, the people I've contacted are telling me they want to see a real star."

Liam nodded thoughtfully. "I guess it's a sign of

imes, isn't it? People do love their celebrities. Harry, when's the latest you can put out some tising if we're able to secure a bigger headline act the boys' choir?"

f I know by the next meeting, I can get the new ts printed in time."

lright then." Liam swiveled his head in Paige's tion. "Miss Ridley, that gives you two weeks to us a celebrity to perform in the show."

Two...I'm sorry, did you say me?" Paige's heart ded in alarm.

Of course! You're the professional musician, after Liam laughed. "If any of us knew how to book a rity musical act, we'd have done it already." A tering of chuckles echoed throughout the room.

aige nodded, stunned. *What have I gotten myself* Two weeks to find a headline act in a foreign try where her circle of contacts didn't stretch h beyond one queer lady farmer, her loyal canine panion, and a lackadaisical guard llama? This was n of events she hadn't seen coming.

retting over the whole debacle, Paige slid behind wheel of the car and eased the plastic boot from foot so that she could operate the pedals. She'd dy learned the hard way on the church organ that s and pedals do not mix. *What does the committee I'm going to do, whip out my super-secret black book of nationally famous music people and just open to a random and call someone?* She wondered exactly how that

was supposed to work. *Hello? Sir Elton John? What c*
have going on for Christmas Eve... But she'd promis
help and she didn't want to let them down.

She was so worked up about her predicament
she drove the entire mile back to the cottage o
wrong side of the road. Being an American, it fel
the right side to her, plus the road was most
narrow that it couldn't be said, strictly speakin
have more than one side. She didn't realize her
until she spun around the corner to head up the
to the cottage and nearly took out an oncoming
Fingers clenched and adrenaline pumping, she p
in front of her cottage and shut off the engine, pra
she would never need to operate a vehicle in
country again.

She took a step toward the front walkway,
paused as she heard a very canine sounding whir
in the distance. Up the road, she saw Maxine stan
on her hind legs and pawing at Fiona's front door
some urgency. Frowning, Paige crossed the stree
check it out.

"Maxie? What's the matter girl?" The little
panted happily when she heard Paige's voice. '
Fiona leave and forget to unlatch your doggie doo
you?"

Paige looked around and her frown deepe
Fiona's car was still parked in the drive and
untouched newspaper sat on the front step. By
looks of it, Fiona hadn't gone anywhere. *But if that'*

case, why hasn't she heard Maxine's scratching and let her in? Balling up her fist, Paige pounded insistently on the door. Relief washed over her as she heard the metallic click of a bolt unlatching inside. The hinges squeaked as the door opened a crack and Maxine scooted inside. When Fiona's face appeared, Paige gasped.

"Fiona! Are you okay?"

The woman's usually tan skin had taken on a waxy pallor and there were dark circles under her eyes. She moaned and leaned against the door frame weakly, shaking her head. "Oh, Paige. I'm not well."

Without pausing to think, Paige stepped into the house and scooped Fiona into her arms, bustling her to the nearest place to lie down. She grabbed a blanket from one of the chairs and, just as Fiona had done for her, she tucked it around her as tightly as she could. Beneath the soft wool, she could feel Fiona's body shake and her skin felt like it was on fire. "I think you have the flu," she said, deep lines creasing her forehead.

Fiona nodded. "I'm so cold."

"Should I make some tea?" Paige scratched her head as Fiona made a repulsed face. "No, okay. No tea. How about soup? I make a chicken soup that can cure anything."

Fiona smiled weakly. "That sounds nice, but it's too much trouble."

Paige waved away her concern. "I just need to get a few ingredients. Is there a grocery store nearby?"

"A few miles. You'd have to drive."

Paige cringed at the suggestion. "What about at the Black Fleece? Do you think I could borrow what I need from Maria?"

Fiona nodded, and Paige wrapped her arms tightly around her. "Okay. Then I'll be back in an hour. You rest until then." With a kiss to Fiona's fevered forehead, Paige headed out the door, sad that Fiona was ill, but humming with joy at the prospect of helping her get well.

AS SOON AS Paige explained to Maria that Fiona was sick, the cook had bundled up every ingredient and cooking implement that she could possibly require, and Paige had soon been heading back up to her cottage to make her magical cure. With soup made and eaten, and Fiona resting comfortably, Paige wasn't sure what to do next. It felt strange to sit and watch the woman sleep, after all, and sleep was what she needed most. Paige's presence was likely to be more of a distraction than a help. Finally, she decided to gather up the supplies she hadn't used and return them to the Black Fleece.

When she entered the kitchen her nostrils were teased with all the scents of Christmas. Cinnamon and cloves, citrus and ginger. Maria stood at the counter, her long braid tucked up into a hairnet, stirring the contents of a huge metal bowl with a thick wooden spoon. She turned as Paige entered the room.

"How's Fiona?"

Paige smiled reassuringly, touched by the cook's obvious concern. "Resting. What is that you're making? It smells heavenly!"

"Christmas pudding!"

"So soon? Christmas is still a month away."

"You have to make them early. I'll steam them today and then soak them in brandy until we serve them on Christmas day. Here, give it a stir and make a wish." She held out the long-handled spoon so that Paige could take hold.

Paige stuck the spoon into the bowl of lumpy batter and paused. "A wish?"

"It's supposed to be good luck."

Paige closed her eyes and tried to think, but she was too distracted by the image of Fiona's faced that formed behind her closed lids to think of anything that she wanted. Finally, she opened her eyes and stirred anyway. Maybe she could bank the unused wish for another time. "So, is the Black Fleece expecting a big turnout for Christmas dinner this year?"

Maria shook her head sadly. "It's been better."

"Fiona told me that business wasn't so good lately." Paige chewed her lip thoughtfully. "Why do you think that is? Fiona thought it was because she's an outsider, that maybe the locals don't want to come here now that Alice is gone. Do you think that's true?"

Maria's eyes narrowed as she considered her answer. "If that's part of it, it's only a very small part. I was born in Portugal, myself. And my father's from Brazil. Even though I don't have blond hair and pink cheeks, I've never felt like anyone thought less of me for it. And Brandon's from Scotland, and he's friends with every man in the village." Maria shrugged. "We all started as outsiders, but she's the only one who feels like one."

"And it wouldn't be homophobia, would it?"

Maria shook her head. "Oh, I don't think so. The people around here knew Alice from the time she was a baby. They loved her, and if she loved Fiona, well, that was that. Not saying they're perfect, but I can't think of a single villager who wouldn't have gone and danced at their wedding."

Paige nodded, her heart squeezed by an uncomfortable mix of sadness and jealousy. "It sounds like Alice was a really special person."

"Oh, she was, the poor lamb. She had a heart of gold." As Maria brushed a tear from her cheek with the back of her hand, Paige found that she was glad to hear it. Fiona deserved to have been loved by someone like that. *Even if it would make it that much harder to compete...*

Paige brushed the thought away. She had no intention of trying to compete. "So if that's not it, what do you think is behind the Black Fleece's troubles?" she asked, conveniently changing the subject.

"For one thing, this place is out-of-date. I've been here since Alice's father ran things, and not much changed for way too long. Same old menu, same tired decor. Alice had a lot of ideas, but she died before she could carry them out. And Fiona's been too caught up in her grief to do anything."

It tore at her heart to picture Fiona hobbled by her loss. She'd seen a glimpse now and then of pain beneath her surface, but either she mostly hid it well, or her outlook transformed when Paige was around. Paige wished it might be the latter, but was afraid to believe it. One thing was certain, the condition of the pub's interior gave weight to the severity of Fiona's paralysis. Though cozy and inviting, she'd noticed right away that the pub gave off an old-fashioned vibe, and not in a cool retro way. It wouldn't take a style guru to know this place needed an extreme makeover, ASAP. "Would it be hard to change?"

"The menu's already changing. At least Fiona's finally come around to that. Now it's just the challenge of getting the word out."

"Honestly, Maria, the food's amazing. I've played in a lot of bars in my time, and your cooking blows them all away. You just need a hook, something to get people back in the door…" Her voice trailed off as her words echoed in her mind. *That's what's missing!* Paige's eyes lit up in excitement. "A piano! That's what would get people coming in. How many places in the area have live music?"

Maria raised her eyebrows. "Live music? Not any that I can think of. But how are we going to get a piano in here? And who would play it if we did?"

Paige grinned, a plan rapidly taking shape. "Do you think Brandon could round up a few strong friends and meet me up at the cottage? I know exactly where we can find a piano, and someone to play it, too!"

Maria laughed. "I'll hunt him down as soon as the puddings are steaming. But do you think we should ask Fiona about this first?"

"She needs her rest. I think we should see if it works, and then surprise her with it if it does."

Maria gave her a long look, her face softening as she did. "You're a lot like her in that way, you know. The ideas, and the energy."

"Like who?"

"Alice. She always had a vision for how things should be, and she'd make it happen. Fiona needs that."

"That's kind of you to say." Tears stung Paige's eyes. She was flattered by the comparison, but also troubled. Mostly, she was honored. From all she'd seen, Alice had been universally loved and admired. But deep down, it made Paige question whether the connection she felt between Fiona and her was unique to them, or the result of Fiona being drawn to her as a substitute for Alice.

"I think it's wonderful that you two have found each other."

Paige's cheeks flushed scarlet. "We're not...I mean, it isn't..."

Maria shrugged and gave a knowing smile. "Whatever you say. Here, keep stirring this and I'll go find Brandon."

An hour later, the old upright piano had been loaded onto a wagon and gently wheeled down the hill and into the pub. Paige cleared a spot for it by the bar, then sat at the stool and pounded out a lively ragtime song. "We're in luck! It sounds like it stayed in tune." She grinned as a couple of the locals who were having a drink by the fire clapped in appreciation. "Come back this evening," she called out to them, "and let your friends know there will be live music at dinner at the Black Fleece tonight!"

After checking in on Fiona and finding with relief that her fever had broken while she slept, Paige went back to her cottage to change into something nice to perform in. Her eyes rested on the empty space in the living room where the piano had been. She felt a momentary pang of guilt over Mike's movie, which was almost certainly not going to get a score composed for it with the piano now residing down the hill, but it was quickly replaced by giddiness over the thought of playing for an audience. Even a very small audience would be exciting. It was what had drawn her to music in the first place. Besides, if anyone from the church happened to hear her play, it would be nice if they would spread the word that she wasn't a complete hack.

As it turned out, the audience at the Black Fleece was not small at all. The locals from the afternoon turned out to be some of the more prolific gossips in town, and news of the Black Fleece piano spread like wildfire. By eight that evening, every table was filled and the tip jar on the bar was overflowing. Though Paige doubted it would be legal for her to keep the money in it on her tourist visa, the pleasure it gave her just to know that people had enjoyed her music was worth much more. By the end of the night, Paige had even been approached by a few other local musicians who were looking for a place to play. With a little organization, music nights at the Black Fleece could go on long after she'd returned to the states.

It was almost midnight when she made it back up the hill, stopping first to change into some warm sweats, then continuing up to check on Fiona. When she let herself into the farmhouse, Fiona was lounging on the couch, weak but awake.

"How are you feeling?"

"Tired," Fiona replied. "But better. That soup really was a miracle cure."

Paige grinned. "Good, I'm glad. Do you want help getting up to your room to sleep?"

Fiona shook her head. "I'm okay here. Besides, you still have your ankle to think of."

"You're right. We're both a mess."

"You can keep me company down here, though, if you'd like." Fiona patted the cushion beside her and Paige took a seat, adjusting her body so that Fiona could curl up with her head in her lap just as Paige had done before. "It's so late! You must have managed to keep yourself occupied today just fine without me!"

Paige chuckled as she thought back over the day. She couldn't remember the last time she'd been so busy or accomplished so much. For the first time in over a year, she felt like herself. It was exhausting and wonderful. She couldn't wait to tell Fiona all about it, but later, when she was well. For now, she closed her eyes and rested her head against the sofa behind her, and focused on the sensation in the tips of her fingers as she ran them through Fiona's dark, silky hair.

TWELVE

"THESE SEATS ARE UNBELIEVABLE!" Paige exclaimed, her eyes glistening as she looked around the gilded interior of Harrogate's Royal Hall. "How did you get them again?"

"I called in a favor from a friend." Fiona kept a tight grasp on Paige's elbow as she escorted her down the crowded aisle in the orchestra seating area. Though Dr. Ross had given the all-clear to dispense with the walking boot and crutches, Fiona didn't want Paige taking unnecessary chances and getting trampled. And truthfully, after three days in bed with the flu, Fiona was still a little unsteady herself and needed the support from Paige's arm as much as Paige needed hers.

They inched right past the merely decent seats and went straight for the truly impressive ones, about 10 rows back from the stage and directly in the center.

Impressive was a relative term, of course. This venue was just a fraction of the size of the Royal Albert in London, where Fiona had performed in the national competition the previous year. It was no Sydney Opera House, either. But for a venue in Yorkshire, it was one of the best; a beautifully restored Edwardian-era theater that attracted world-class talent on a regular basis. A holiday symphony was the last place she wanted to be, filled as it was with ghosts of a life she'd put behind her, but it was worth it to repay Paige's kindness.

"That must have been some friend," Paige commented as she edged her way into their row and scooted past the people who were already seated there. "I heard the tickets have been sold out for months!"

Fiona tilted her head by way of acknowledgment, but said nothing. She'd simply rung up Philip, of course, or rather she'd finally returned one of the periodic voicemails he left that she usually just ignored. *Two tickets to the annual holiday symphony? Consider it done! And while I have you on the phone, isn't it time that we talked about staging your global comeback tour?* The strange thing was, she'd suddenly found herself not entirely opposed to the idea. She hadn't said yes, but she hadn't exactly said no, either. Something told her that she had the woman sitting next to her to thank—or blame—for that.

Maybe it had been the tales of Paige's musical triumphs at the Black Fleece this past week that had inspired Fiona to reconsider her self-imposed retirement. Paige's bubbling enthusiasm, both for her own performances and for the growing number of local musicians who had approached her to schedule gigs, was infectious. Her nightly accounts of what she had played and how the audience had reacted had given Fiona a vicarious thrill, and made her wonder if she'd made the decision to retire a bit too hastily.

Because she'd been ill, Fiona hadn't had a chance to make it to the pub to see the changes Paige had made, but she was grateful for them. It had torn Fiona apart to see Alice's pub in decline, but deep down, she was humble enough to admit that she hadn't the first idea what to do about it. The fact that Paige had come around and made this happen, seemingly without effort, felt like a godsend to her.

The other thing her recent illness had curtailed was a proper discussion about what had happened between them at the parade Sunday night. *The Kiss*. She'd been too sick on Monday to think about it. On Tuesday, her fever had returned and Paige had slept beside her all that night to keep watch over her. Discussing kissing while the party in question lay just inches away in the same bed had seemed the height of awkwardness, so she'd put it off. By Wednesday, the thought of bringing it up had made Fiona squirm from head to toe. *Why bother?* They seemed to have survived her momentary lapse in judgment with their friendship intact, so Fiona wasn't so certain anymore that there was a need to dissect the details.

In the red velvet seat beside her, Paige was flipping through the pages of the evening's program. "Oh! Sarah Tillson's singing tonight. Do you know her?"

"Sarah Tillson? Know her?" Fiona held back a snort. *Know her?* They'd been part of the Royal Opera's artist in residence program together, gone to some of the same parties. She'd once helped hold Sarah's hair back after a particularly wild night ended with her puking in the alley behind a club in the East End. Saucy Sarah, they'd called her, partially due to her fondness for drinks and partially because of her willingness to say anything or do pretty much whatever she pleased.

"Oh! You're looking at me funny. Does what I said not mean the same thing here that it means back home?" Paige's hands fluttered around her cheeks. "I've spoken English my entire life, but since I got here, I've felt like I'm saying everything wrong! I meant have you *heard* of her. I hadn't, but I read about her in the in-flight magazine on the way to London. Oh, God! I hope I didn't imply that I was asking if you *knew* her in, like in the *Biblical* sense of the word."

Fiona gaped. She had it on good authority that while Sarah usually went out with men, she'd been known to make exceptions to that rule after a few too many martinis from time to time, but she didn't have direct evidence one way or the other. *Ah, Saucy Sarah.*

Good times. Meanwhile, Paige's hilariously flustered rambling was absolutely killing her. "Well, I've never had *that* pleasure," she teased, "but I may have *heard* of her, yes."

Paige folded her hands in her lap primly. "She's a mezzo-soprano."

Fiona nodded. *Yes she is, and bitter about it, too. Always complaining that the roles for mezzos were second-rate, telling me how she'd be as big a star as I was if only people recognized the true beauty of a mezzo's range...*

Paige frowned. "That means that her voice is a little bit lower, somewhere between a soprano and a contralto."

Fiona's stomach tightened nervously as she realized that Paige had mistaken her silence for a lack of knowledge. *I really need to tell her.* She'd kept quiet about her history in the beginning thinking it was easier that way. She didn't like to talk about her past with anyone, least of all a stranger passing through, which was how Paige had started out. And then she'd figured that the last thing she needed when trying to keep a safe emotional distance between Paige and herself was to admit just how much they had in common. But the longer they knew each other and the closer they became, the more Fiona realized that it was something she needed to explain, before her omission started looking like a lie.

"Paige, there's something—" As she began to speak, the houselights dimmed and the sound of strings and woodwinds warming up echoed through the auditorium as the buzz of talking ceased. Fiona stopped mid-sentence and closed her mouth. She could explain it all after the show.

As the concert began, Fiona increasingly found her eyes drifting surreptitiously from the musicians on stage to the companion at her side. That Fiona found Paige attractive wasn't a secret. Her bold and quirky appearance had won Fiona over from the start, those glasses that hid her smoky gray eyes, and that aubergine hair—which, Fiona noted, had started to fade to a lovely lavender now. It all stoked a physical desire inside her that burned unceasingly whenever Paige was near. But that wasn't why she watched her now. Fiona was engrossed by the lively glow of her enthusiasm. The emotion playing out across her fair features stirred feelings inside her that Fiona had believed to be gone for good. It was both wonderful and troubling.

The combination of Paige and music created magic. Watching Paige smile during a crescendo or close her eyes to immerse herself in a soloist's voice was like watching the first bulbs spring up, fresh and green after the frost of winter. Her face held the secret promise of brighter days, and just by being near her Fiona felt warmth and hope in parts of her that, since Alice's death, had only known cold and despair. Fiona's voice had been frozen, but Paige made her want to sing. It's why she'd kissed her at the Christmas parade. It's why she couldn't take her eyes off her now. And she had no idea what to do about it.

Fiona trained her eyes on the stage, hoping to clear her thoughts. Almost as soon as she did, she felt the brush of velvety skin against her inner elbow as Paige hooked her arm around Fiona's atop the armrest between their seats. Paige drew closer, her head coming to rest on Fiona's shoulder, and Fiona felt an irresistible pull toward her, until her own head was nestled against Paige's. Remaining just friends for the next month seemed an unlikely option. A future beyond that was impossible. Could the time they had left be enough?

The concert ended in amid thunderous applause. As Fiona and Paige rose to leave, Fiona could just make out the sound of someone shouting her name over the din. She looked in the direction it had come from and saw Philip barreling toward her, beaming from ear to ear.

"Fiona! There you are!"

Fiona's heart clenched. "Philip! What are you doing here?" She knew, of course. In her eagerness to show Paige a good time, she'd left herself wide open. Philip was too good at what he did to have the knowledge of exactly when and where to find her and not put it to use.

"Who could pass up Harrogate for the holidays?" Odds were good Philip had never seen Harrogate before in his life. "And who is this lovely lady you have with you?"

Fiona turned to Paige, who watched the exchange in polite confusion. "Paige, this is my..." Given that she still hadn't had a chance to explain her previous career as an overnight international singing sensation to Paige, she struggled with how to describe him. "This is Philip. Philip, Paige. Philip's the one who got us the tickets for this evening," she added.

A broad smile split Paige's face. "It's a pleasure to meet you! Thank you so much."

"Anytime! It was worth it for me to have this chance to talk with Fiona. She can be very elusive when she wants to be."

"Unfortunately, Philip, we need to be heading back. It's a long drive back to Holme and it's already getting late."

"Now Fiona, I wouldn't hear of it," he scolded, taking her by the arm as Paige followed. "Not when there are at least a hundred people up at the hotel for the annual Christmas party who are just dying to see you."

"Philip." There was a subtle warning in Fiona's tone. Having Philip corner her at the concert was one thing. She'd brought that on herself by coming here. But she had no desire to socialize with others from her old life.

"I won't take no for an answer, Fiona." His words were congenial but firm. "As for the drive, I've already booked you a room for the night." He glanced at Paige and lowered his voice meaningfully. "Two beds, or one. Your choice. Just let the front desk know which is more appropriate."

Fiona could feel hot blood racing to her cheeks at Philip's insinuation, and a flutter inside her belly as she imagined the shock facing Paige when they arrived at the hotel to find a ballroom filled with people who all knew Fiona's name. She broke away from Philip and looped her arm around Paige's waist, leaning close to her ear. "Paige, Philip's invited us to a party." Fiona took a deep breath as Paige looked expectantly at her. "Look, there's something I should probably explain…"

WALKING a step or two behind Fiona and Philip, Paige shivered as a gust of icy wind whipped across the expansive hotel grounds, the entrance to which was just steps from Royal Hall. The massive Victorian structure ahead stood dark against the inky sky, but from a ballroom on the ground floor came the sounds of music and laughter, and the golden glow of chandeliers. It was the last place she'd expected to wind up tonight.

Fiona had attempted to explain what was going on, but Paige had quickly become so confused that the details failed to make any sense. *A professional singer? Fiona?* And one who was so internationally renowned that every person at the party they were headed to would recognize her on sight. Paige thought of the moment earlier in the evening when she'd tried to explain what a mezzo-soprano was, and embarrassment consumed her.

She must have thought I was an idiot! And yet, this was still the same Fiona as before, the same woman she knew. The one who owned a farm, and a llama. The one who'd kissed her at the Christmas parade until her toes started to tingle, and sometimes stole glances at her that made Paige feel like she was the most beautiful woman in the world. The one with the strawberry shaped birthmark at the top of her inner thigh that made her laugh until she lost her breath when it was stroked with the tip of a wet tongue. *And I'll bet that's something no one else here knows about the world-famous Fiona Blake!* She frowned as she followed Fiona through the front door and into the marble-lined lobby. *At least, I hope no one does!*

A million questions bubbled up in her mind, but it went exactly like Fiona had predicted. Two steps in the door, with a wordless apology contained in her backward glance, Fiona was whisked away as dozens of people called out her name. Nerves jangling from the surprising turn of events, Paige went in search of the bar.

"Paige?"

With a sharp intake of breath, Paige realized that she knew that voice. *But what is she doing here?* "Veronica?" Sure enough, she spun on her heels to find her ex girlfriend standing just inches behind her. "What... how are you—"

"I'm representing the BASO at the music consortium conference in town. I had no idea you would be here."

Paige shrank beneath the weight of accusation behind her words. Whether she was upset that Paige was there, or mad at her for not telling her where she was going, Paige wasn't sure. She just knew that Veronica was displeased. Old habits left her feeling duty-bound to make it right. "I'm sorry, Veronica. I've been—"

"Oh. My. God." Veronica's mouth gaped as she stared past Paige. "Is that Fiona Blake? I heard a rumor she might be here, but I didn't believe it!"

"Wait. How do you know—"

"Oh, that's right," Veronica interrupted. "You don't keep up on anything beyond your jazz music." She said the word jazz dismissively, as if it were on par with boy bands and bubblegum pop. "You wouldn't know who that is. She's a singer, world-renowned, and a *total* mystery."

Paige's eyebrows shot up, her interest piqued. "How's that?"

"A year ago in Sydney, she won the top prize in the most prestigious vocal music contest on the planet. It's the type of thing a singer dreams of. Winners pretty much have it made."

Paige nodded eagerly, suddenly glad to have run into Veronica who, though a violinist herself, kept up on most of the gossip throughout the wider music world. "And then?"

"Poof! She disappeared. It was a few weeks before Thanksgiving. I remember because I was watching the competition on TV while looking for apartments." To hear this painful reminder of their breakup referenced so casually made Paige draw in a sharp breath, but Veronica continued without seeming to notice. "They'd just announced that she would be performing at the gala at the Sydney Opera House on New Year's Eve and then, nothing. She was just gone. She withdrew from the gala and hasn't performed in public since. No one knows why."

Paige knew why. *Alice.* That was right around the time that Alice had gotten sick. With a sinking feeling, Paige wondered if Fiona had been in Sydney when Alice got the news. If so, she must have been consumed by guilt to have not been by her side. *No wonder she couldn't face performing after that.*

"But anyway, what are you doing here, Paige? I didn't even know you were in the UK!" Veronica looked past Paige as she spoke, her eyes tracking Fiona at the other end of the room.

"I'm on sabbatical, I guess you could say." Paige squared her shoulders as she said it, liking how official that word felt. *Sabbatical.* So much better than saying she fled the country to avoid a mental breakdown due to the woman now standing in front of her.

Veronica nodded absently, her attention still focused on Fiona the throng that surrounded her.

Paige's inability to get her to listen rankled, and she searched for a topic that would engage her ex's attention. "As it happens, I've been asked to head up a Christmas music festival for a charity event in a few weeks."

"Uh huh?"

"Lots of responsibility. In fact, I'm here tonight to see if I can recruit one last act for the show. We're looking for a real headliner." While that had nothing to do with why Paige was there, the idea had popped into her head and sounded impressive enough to get Veronica to make eye contact with her, so she went with it. Mulling it over now, Paige felt a rush of excitement. She was in a room full of some of the best musicians in England. She'd accidentally stumbled upon a pretty solid idea!

Veronica's face lit up with excitement as her eyes drifted back to Paige. "Oh my God!"

Paige's cheeks flushed with pride. "Well, I—"

"She's coming over here!" Veronica smoothed her face to hide the fangirl within, as Paige slumped with the realization that Veronica still wasn't paying attention. "Wow, she's kinda hot, too. You know, I've heard rumors that she—"

"Paige!" Fiona called out in a stage whisper, motioning with one hand for Paige to come closer.

Veronica's jaw dropped. "You *know* her? How do you know her?"

"Excuse me, Veronica." Paige turned and walked toward Fiona without additional explanation.

"Paige, it looks like I'm going to be stuck in here most of the night." Fiona held out her hand and gave Paige a key card. "We're in room 207. It has two beds, so no worries."

Paige nodded, ignoring the sense of deflation that hit her at that news. *One bed would have been a happy mistake.*

"You don't mind staying, do you? We can head home now if you'd rather."

"No, it's fine. In fact, I ran into someone—"

"You mean that woman you've been talking to nonstop over there who keeps staring so strangely at me?"

If she didn't know better, Paige would have sworn that Fiona sounded jealous that they'd been talking before. She smiled slyly. "You mean Veronica?"

"Oh, is that her name? Veronica." She said it like the name tasted unpleasant on her tongue. Then her face clouded. "Wait, wasn't Veronica the name—"

"Of the girlfriend who dumped me? The very same."

Fiona arched an eyebrow. "I see. Maybe I should go

say thank you. Without her, you wouldn't have come here. And we never would have...*met*." She looked Paige up and down hungrily and grinned a naughty grin.

Paige felt a wave of heat rush through her at both the boldness and the intimacy of the moment. It was clear Fiona had been thinking specifically of the first night they'd met when she said it, and was busy picturing a repeat performance. And it would probably be obvious to anyone in the room who saw them right now, too. Paige frowned, wondering why Fiona was willing to risk adding fuel to the already active rumor mill that surrounded them. Then she saw Fiona sneak a satisfied glance at Veronica, and a thrill rippled through her. *She's trying to make Veronica jealous!*

Someone called for Fiona from across the room and the heat in her eyes evaporated. "I'd better go. Remember, room 207. I'll be up when I can."

Why couldn't there have been just one bed?

Veronica stood wide-eyed at her return. "Paige Ridley! Are you here with Fiona Blake? Are you two *dating?*"

She'd nearly shouted the last part, and Paige cringed. "Veronica, *shhh*. No, we're not dating. I'm renting her brother's cottage while I'm in town."

Veronica nodded. "Right. While you're in town organizing the music festival. Which I'd love to star in, of course! I'm so glad we're still close enough that you felt comfortable asking me."

Paige stared. She hadn't asked her anything! "Starring in the festival?"

"You said you needed a big name. And I *am* a fairly accomplished violinist, I don't mind saying. I knew that's what you were warming up to ask. I know you, Paige-y. Remember?"

Paige bristled involuntarily at the old nickname. "I remember, Veronica." *I remember that there's usually something you're after for yourself as soon you call me that!*

"So, is your friend Fiona going to be performing, too? Maybe we could work together on something."

And that's what she was after. Of course. Starstruck Veronica would do anything to rub elbows with someone who might further her career. The joke was on her, though, since Fiona had nothing to do with the concert.

Paige chewed on her bottom lip, it suddenly occurring to her to question exactly why that might be. She'd taken Fiona's lack of involvement at face value, but that was before she'd discovered that Fiona was a world-famous singer. She was exactly the type of big name that the committee was desperate for to head up the show. A show that was raising money for charity in the memory of her beloved girlfriend, Alice. So why hadn't she volunteered?

"Paige-y? Are you listening to me?" Veronica pouted until Paige made eye contact. "That's better. I've been so worried about you, you know. When you didn't come by last month after you said you would, I didn't know what to think."

Paige raised an eyebrow, regarding her with skepticism. If she'd been so worried, she might have tried calling. Or texting. Or an email. Still, the thought of her feeling concerned was appealing.

"I've really missed you, Paige." As she said it, Veronica brushed her finger along Paige's cheek and down to the hollow of her throat. Paige swallowed, knowing if she didn't stop her, she'd soon be sliding that finger deep into Paige's cleavage.

"I've thought about it a lot lately," Veronica continued. Her finger descended to around mid-chest. "In fact, I think when you get back home, we should get together and talk about things. I mean, unless you wanted to come up to my room here tonight and…talk?"

It was everything Paige had dreamed of hearing for the past year, yet the words left her feeling oddly annoyed. *Was she always like this?* She'd shifted so quickly from bored to flirtatious that Paige was afraid she'd get whiplash.

Paige shook her head and took a step back, leaving Veronica's finger suspended in midair. "I don't think tonight's a good time, Veronica." Paige was firm in her response. She couldn't believe how manipulative Veronica could be! *And yet, she's saying everything I want to hear…* "When I get back, though. Maybe." She hated not being able to resist leaving that last part off, but she couldn't help herself. After all this time, Veronica still held just enough sway over her that she couldn't cut her off completely. *I guess you don't get over all that history in just a few weeks.* "Right now, I'm heading to bed."

As she climbed the grand, curved staircase to her room, she couldn't help but wonder at the curveball fate had thrown her. A month ago, she would have jumped at Veronica's thinly veiled offer of sex in exchange for a social status and career boost. She would have convinced herself that it was love. Maybe even destiny, especially finding Veronica *again*, across the ocean and so close to Christmas. Instead she'd chosen to spend the night in twin beds with a woman who kept secrets. And she'd try to convince herself that it wasn't love, because it couldn't be. Why couldn't anything ever go according to plan?

THIRTEEN

"SO THAT WAS VERONICA, WAS IT?" Fiona's grip on the steering wheel tightened as she pictured the woman in her mind. *Pretty, I guess, but nothing special.* There'd been something about her that she didn't like, though.

"In the flesh." Paige, who'd silently been watching the Yorkshire landscape roll by the passenger's window on the drive from Harrogate back to Holme, turned her head toward Fiona. She looked as conflicted over the woman's surprise appearance as Fiona felt.

"And she's really coming to Holme to perform at the Christmas festival?" Fiona's fingers clenched again as Paige nodded. "You're sure that's a good idea? I mean, she is the reason you came all this way. To get *away* from her."

Paige shrugged. "It's okay. Besides, I did need to find a headline act for the program. Veronica's a fairly well respected violinist. Not famous, but the types of people who were at the symphony last night would know who she is and be willing to travel to hear her, I think. Under the circumstances, I'm not sure I could do better."

"Do you want me to make a few calls? I do know some people."

Paige snorted. "So I noticed."

Fiona's stomach dropped. "Paige, I'm really sorry about springing it on you like that. I was going to explain the whole thing, I swear, just as soon as we were in the car heading home last night. I had no idea Philip would be there, let alone that he'd drag us to that party." *Not to mention the staying overnight, and the room with the twin beds…and God, why did this have to be such torture?* They'd barely had a chance to talk since the concert ended, and Fiona was terrified that Paige was mad at her.

"It's okay, Fee. I understand."

When Paige used her nickname, Fiona's spirits soared. She'd been surrounded by old friends at the party and Paige must have heard them all calling her that, but the fact that she'd started saying it too just felt so right.

"As for Veronica," Paige continued, "that's okay, too, I think. I appreciate you being willing to reach out on my behalf, but Veronica will be fine. And it was generous of her to offer."

"Yes, that seems…" Fiona hesitated. Given her

initial impression of the woman, and what she'd gleaned from Paige in the past, her willingness to pitch in seemed almost *too* generous. But Fiona didn't want to point it out the wrong way and upset Paige.

Paige's brow furrowed as she waited for Fiona to continue.

"Well, I don't know her like you do. She just struck me as the type who doesn't offer her services unless there's something in it to compensate for it."

Paige chuckled, relaxing. "That's very perceptive. You can't imagine how many years it's taken for me to figure that out."

"Maybe..." Fiona felt all the muscles in her body constrict. "You don't suppose she's still interested in you, do you?"

Paige shook her head and Fiona's shoulder's sagged in relief. "No, no way. I mean, I don't think..." Paige looked away, once again watching the deserted fields roll by. Finally she drew in a breath and spoke. "Fee, can I ask you something? Why did you quit?"

"You mean why did I quit my music career?" Fiona sighed heavily. It was a subject she dreaded, but after being exposed to the existence of her former life and handling it so graciously, Paige deserved a better explanation than she'd been given.

"I met Alice when I was in residence at the Royal Opera. She worked in the business office. She wasn't a musician herself, but of course she knew when we met that I was and that I had some pretty grandiose ideas about how I was going to make it big."

"Grandiose?" Paige cocked an eyebrow. "Considering the reaction of the crowd at the party last night, I'm not sure that grandiose is the right word. Seems like you had a pretty realistic view of your chances, and what you needed to do to get there."

Fiona chuckled. "Maybe so. I loved performing, and I was fairly certain I had what it would take to succeed, if that's what you mean. I'm not sure if Alice fully understood at the time what was involved, or how often it would take me away."

Paige nodded encouragingly.

"God, I did love it, though. New cities and new audiences. The competitions. It was so exciting that I didn't even think about what I might be missing at home. I figured it would always be there, you know? I was in Sydney when I got the news that Alice was sick. I rushed home as soon as I heard, but…" *But she died without ever knowing I was there.* Fiona kept that last secret in. It was too shameful to share. "And then, I don't know. I guess I just lost my passion for it. When Philip approached me early in the new year, I just couldn't go back. He's been trying ever since, but nothing's changed."

"Even now?" Paige studied her pensively, and deep down even Fiona questioned if that was true. "You really seemed to be enjoying yourself last night."

She *had* been having fun, and now she felt awful for

it. Her Pavlovian response of guilt was so automatic that it seemed natural. *But is that really how it should be?* "I don't know. It was nice to be back with friends and be a part of that world again, but there's still something missing. I don't feel the inspiration like I used to."

"I understand. I felt like that, too, right up until I started playing at the Black Fleece this week."

"So, do you think it's possible to get it back?" Fiona's pulse ticked up in anticipation of Paige's response. Could there actually be hope of kicking the guilt and finding the joy she'd lost again someday?

"I do. At least in part. Don't get me wrong, not everything is back to normal. When it comes to getting that stupid film score I'm supposed to be working on done, I'm as stuck as ever."

With a wry grin, Paige turned back to watching the scenery while Fiona drove. They were just passing a grove of pine trees when Paige remarked, "You know what you need? A Christmas tree."

Fiona considered it, but something about a festively decorated tree didn't fit with her drab living room. "With my luck, Maxie would pee all over it."

"I wasn't thinking for your house. I was thinking of the Black Fleece. You're still undersold for Christmas dinner, you know. Maybe seeing a big, sparkling tree will inspire people to book ahead."

"How big were you thinking? Because I understand that *someone* has just moved a piano into my pub."

Fiona chuckled at Paige's exasperated look. "You have more ideas for that place than I do, you know. It's a shame it's not your pub, because I think you'd do a better job of running it." She shook her head, surprised by the sudden tingle of anticipation she felt at the prospect of decorating the Fleece for the holidays. "Alright. Let's get a tree."

Paige wiggled her shoulders and torso in a little dance of excitement. "Really? What do you think, maybe an artificial one with those pre-lit LED lights?"

"That is the most American thing I've ever heard. This is the Yorkshire countryside, darling. We can do better than that. Your ankle is better and I'm over the flu. We should celebrate. We'll cut down our own!" Fiona felt her own excitement building. After too much time cooped inside, it would be an adventure to walk through the crisp air with Paige, and snuggle close together for warmth. And maybe just a little bit romantic, too. *And would that be such a bad thing?*

"We can bring the tree back to the pub and then have some piping hot coffee!"

Fiona frowned. "Shouldn't that be hot chocolate?"

"Maybe for you. Personally, I haven't had nearly enough coffee since I got here. I'd do just about anything for a fresh pot!"

When they arrived at the farm, Fiona and Paige parted ways long enough to change into some warm clothes and take advantage of the remaining hours of sunlight. They met up again outside the farmhouse.

"Will we drive?" Paige asked.

"No, for the patch of trees I have in mind, it's better to walk. We just need to stop in the barn for the wagon to help carry it back."

Paige grinned. "Maybe we should take Dolly to help us pull it?"

Fiona shook her head with a laugh. "Are you kidding? Maxine will be beside herself if we do."

The barn sat a ways behind the farmhouse, and the women walked toward it as they talked. As they entered, laughing merrily, they heard a gruff shout from deep inside the building.

"Hello? Fiona, is that you? I need some help!"

"Brandon?" The smile faded from Fiona's lips at the serious tone in the caretaker's voice.

"Yeah, I'm back here with a ewe that's gone into labor."

Fiona's high spirits plummeted as she raced to the back of the barn. Brandon was on his knees in the straw, comforting the distressed sheep. All around them was stained with blood. From her somewhat limited knowledge, it didn't look good.

"Paige, I have to stay and help. I'm so sorry."

"It's okay," Paige took in the scene, her face etched with concern. "I'll stay too."

PULLING UP A STOOL, Paige sat quietly in the corner

as Fiona rolled up her sleeves and scrubbed her hands and arms, then toweled them dry and put on a pair of latex exam gloves. She prepared efficiently and without any direction from Brandon, who remained with the struggling ewe. Observing her, Paige marveled at Fiona's ability to move between such different worlds, from a lavish party at night to caring for a farm and livestock just hours later. She seemed able to succeed in whatever environment she found herself in, and Paige wondered if she knew what a rare gift that was.

"How did she end up like this?" Fiona asked when she returned. "I thought lambing wasn't usually until the spring."

"She must have got in with the rams in a neighbor's field one of the times the fence was down this summer," Brandon answered, slipping on his own set of gloves, "but I only noticed her condition when we did the breeding last month."

"I just don't understand it." Looking exasperated, Fiona blew a stray strand of hair from in front of her eyes. "That fence was completely replaced. It cost a bloody fortune!"

Brandon nodded. "Still happening, too. I know you don't want to hear it, Fiona, but you'd be better off replacing Dolly with a second dog."

Paige let out a gasp. *Not Dolly!* She'd become fond of the little thing during the llama's frequent visits to her garden. "Are you sure she's to blame? She seems so gentle."

Fiona smiled reassuringly. "Don't worry, Paige. I like Dolly, too. She won't be going anywhere unless she has to." She worked while she talked, holding the ewe firmly as Brandon conducted an internal exam.

"Malpresentation," Brandon said to Fiona. "Front legs only. Keep holding her steady while I search around for the head."

Fiona nodded, clearly understanding his words better than Paige had. "Will you need the snare?"

"Yes, but I need you to keep her still even more."

Fiona looked up. "Paige? Can you go over by the sink and look for something called a lambing snare for me? It's a plastic rod with a handle and a loop, and should be hanging on one of the pegs."

Paige hopped up and retrieved a tool that fit that rough description. "Is this it?" Glimpsing the scene of Brandon with his arm buried inside the ewe, Paige blanched and felt like she might be sick.

"You okay?" Fiona watched her with concern.

"Yeah." Paige shook her head to clear it. "I just need a distraction."

"Did I ever tell you why we have a llama?"

Paige shook her head.

"It was my brother Daniel's idea. There's a farm up north, just past Harrogate, where they raise llamas and make them available for people to take them on walks."

"Walking llamas?" Paige snickered at the mental image that formed in her head. "That's ridiculous!"

"Well, don't knock it until you've tried it. A lot of people really enjoy llama walking, apparently. They sell out weeks ahead sometimes."

Paige's sides ached from giggling. "You're kidding! So why didn't you end up doing it?"

"You've met Dolly. Can you imagine a dozen more just like her? What would Maxine think?"

There was a soft cry like the mewling of a kitten. "There she is," Brandon said in a hushed tone. The sound repeated more loudly, this time sounding more sheep-like.

"Oh my God! Is that the lamb?"

Fiona laughed. "Yes! Was that enough of a distraction for you? It's probably best you didn't watch that part."

"Look at it! It's so tiny!" There was a fullness in her heart as she looked at the newborn lamb, then at Fiona who had handled the situation with such calm and patience alongside Brandon. "That was amazing. Both of you!"

"Lambs usually come in twins," Brandon informed her. "There's one more to come, but it looks routine. I can take over from here."

When Paige looked out the barn door, she discovered that it had grown dark. "It's too late to get that Christmas tree, but how about a dinner at the Black Fleece?"

After a quick change of clothing, they walked down the hill arm in arm. Inside the pub, business was booming. The bar was packed and every table was filled as a local band played from the corner of the room.

"I can't believe this!" Fiona's eyes were wide with shock as she shouted above the music to be heard. "I don't think I've ever seen so many people here. How did you manage it?"

"Inspiration just struck, I guess," Paige explained with a shrug. It had seemed obvious to her at the time, though the result had surpassed her expectations. "This is exactly the type of place I would love to play in back home, so I figured why not here? I'll admit, it turns out there were more aspiring musicians in the valley than I thought, and fewer places for them to play. I've started a calendar, and it's booked well into the new year. You should be able to keep a rotation going long after I leave."

There was a flash of pain in Fiona's eyes at the reminder of how limited their time together would be, and Paige felt it, too. She'd settled into a routine in the village and with Fiona that felt so much like home that it was easy to forget that it was only temporary. The pace of life here suited her, the surroundings and people inspired her. Her joy for music returned a little more each day, and every moment that passed she felt more like herself. She'd come to Holme to figure out how to be happy again, never expecting that what had eluded her in California was waiting in amid a cluster of old stone buildings and rolling pastures that was hardly big enough to find on a map. And the reason for that happiness was becoming more apparent to her with each passing day. *Fiona.*

The connection between them had been electric and immediate on a physical level, and Paige had sensed it was something special even when she'd thought she'd never see Fiona again after one night. And then they'd had the chance to get to know one another, and that feeling had intensified day by day. It was so easy to be with Fiona, to be cared for by her and to take care of her in return. There was a give and take to their relationship that felt natural and sweet, that made Paige feel safe and loved.

Ironically, it had taken seeing Veronica again for Paige to fully appreciate what she'd found in Fiona. With Veronica, Paige always had to be on her toes, guarding against being manipulated, cautious to avoid provoking her anger by saying no. Pleasing Veronica had been the best feeling in the world, but there had always been the knowledge of how easily her mood could turn. Paige's senses were heightened the moment Veronica was in the room, her body buzzing with awareness. But now she realized that it was as much due to self-preservation as attraction. How much of what she'd thought were feelings of love had, in reality, been nothing but her body's natural fight-or-flight instinct?

Sitting snug beside Fiona in the corner table by the roaring fire—*their* table, as Paige always thought of it now—it seemed as impossible that they'd met for the first time in that same spot just a few weeks ago as it did that soon Paige would be flying home. Except for that first night together, they'd been so cautious about forming too close an attachment, as if they both realized how easy it would be to fall in too deep, and how much it would hurt to say goodbye. And yet it was plain as day to Paige that all their precautions were useless. Not sleeping together wouldn't make it hurt any less, not when they'd become so intimate in every other way.

The strains of music from the band, which had provided a temporary substitute for conversation, came to an end and after a smattering of applause, the musicians began packing up their equipment for the night. With a start, Paige realized the lateness of the hour. The tables had cleared of patrons and only a few stragglers drained their last drinks at the bar. She'd passed the evening in a warm, pleasant bubble with Fiona at her side. The harshness of emerging from it sent her searching for something to ease the transition back to reality.

Her eyes landed on the piano, which sat idle now that the band had left, beckoning. Sliding out of her corner seat, Paige went to it and rested her hands on the familiar keys. Her brain lacked a specific plan of what to play, but her fingers had a mind of their own, and soon a familiar Christmas carol echoed through the pub's deserted interior. Lost in the music, Paige closed her eyes and let it flow through her until a crystal clear voice chimed in at the chorus like the sound of an angel.

The shocking beauty of Fiona's voice made her body pulse and her fingers tingle. Her eyes flew open and she stared at Fiona, her own surprise reflected back at her in Fiona's expression, as though she, too, could barely believe that she'd joined in. Enchanted, Paige played to the end of the carol and launched right into another, terrified that if she stopped for even a second, the moment would end. Fiona, who had pulled up a chair beside the piano stool, continued to sing along with increasing confidence, and soon Paige was playing a melody of her own as the inspiration came to her, with Fiona improvising right along. It was a song created between the two of them, a moment of magic just for them.

Finally Paige's fingers slowed and the music ended, and then Fiona was in her arms, pressed tightly against her chest as Paige's heart hammered beneath. As they held each other close, Paige could still hear the music in her head, soon joined by the images that she'd stared at in frustration for weeks. *The film score!* It all came together in a flash, and she knew exactly how it would go. Grinning, she kissed the top of Fiona's head in excitement. Fiona tilted her head upward and Paige kissed her lips with unbridled enthusiasm before she had the chance to say a word.

"What was that for?" Fiona asked, breathless, when they finally parted.

"Inspiration." Paige laughed as Fiona raised her eyebrows in confusion. "I'll explain later. Right now I'd rather kiss you again, if you don't object."

"No, not at all." Fiona melted into her, their bodies working together with the same creative synchronization as their music, creating a moment of magic. "You know, I just live up the hill…" Fiona whispered, the warmth of her breath tickling Paige's ear.

"Oh, is that right?" Paige teased as her body hummed with anticipation. "I bet next you're going to say you have a hankering for a sandwich."

Fiona looked at her in mock surprise. "It's almost like you've heard this pickup line before!"

Paige offered Fiona her hand. "Come on. Maxie's probably wondering what's taking us so long."

As they walked with arms linked up the dark road to the farmhouse, Paige reflected that though the pickup lines may have been the same, tonight was different than before. The first time they'd spent the night together, they were two strangers, struggling to capture a fleeting moment of release in their broken lives. Tonight they were two souls who had found connection and healing in each other. Before, it was about personal pleasure. Tonight was about being in love.

FOURTEEN

FIONA'S EYES remained stubbornly shut as Paige stirred beside her beneath the covers. With one hand gripping the blanket, she pulled it firmly up above her head, shielding her eyes from the sunshine that poured in through the bedroom window. Then she snaked her arm around Paige's waist, pulling her close in the warmth and darkness that surrounded them.

"That's not going to work this time, Fee." Paige's voice was muffled through the covers. "It's time to get up."

"It's Sunday. Getting out of bed on Sunday is optional."

"It's Monday, and the final planning meeting for the Christmas Festival is today. You promised you would come."

How could it be Monday already? Fiona's mind raced back over her memories of the past week, a blur of farm chores quickly completed and every free moment spent exactly like this one, naked and in bed with Paige. It had been the best week of her life. A silly grin spread across her face and was still there a moment later when Paige ripped the covers back, exposing her skin to the cool air.

"Why are you being so mean to me?" Fiona whimpered. At the sound of her distress, she felt Maxine jump up from the foot of the bed and soon found a cold nose and wet tongue covering her face. "Blech!" Doggie kisses weren't exactly the kind she'd had in mind to start off her day, but much to her dismay, Paige had already scooted from the bed and was busy putting on her clothes.

"Come on, Fee. You know I can't miss the meeting. I need to report on Veronica joining the program."

Fiona's nose wrinkled in distaste at the mention of Veronica's name, but it was a reminder to her that if Paige's ex was going to be involved with the festival, it would behoove her to do the same, if only to go to the meeting to get some information for next year. "Fine, you win." She gave Maxine a push and sat upright, swinging her legs to the floor with utmost regret.

The meeting room at the church was buzzing when they arrived, most of the seats already occupied by committee members and local business owners. Fiona's palms grew slick as she looked over the crowd. She recognized almost everyone. Many of them had been customers at the Black Fleece during Alice's tenure, though even in the recent surge of business she didn't recall having seen most of their faces.

They stared back, judging, as she entered the room with Paige. At least that's how Fiona felt under their gaze. Hushed voices reached her ears and her pulse raced. *They're gossiping about us.* With an apologetic look, Fiona took a small step away from Paige, who raised an eyebrow at the move but said nothing. She hoped Paige understood. Everyone in this room had loved Alice, and she was fairly certain most of them disliked her. Putting a little distance between them, quelling the rumors, would be in Paige's best interest even more than her own. But if Paige felt a bit put out by it right now, Fiona didn't blame her. She'd make it up to her later.

The vicar rose to call the meeting to order, but not before doing a double take when he spotted Fiona. She stifled a laugh. She'd managed to avoid running into him since that fateful morning at the house. *That's right, Jonas. I finally dared to show my face.* Funny how she thought of him exclusively by his first name now, and always with that comically shocked expression on his face as his brain tried to make sense of the naked, aubergine-haired goddess who'd fallen into Fiona's garden. She couldn't help it. *I'm definitely going to hell.* She doubted there were many in the room who would disagree.

With few seats to choose from in the crowded room, Fiona had chosen a spot to stand in the rear of the room while Paige had found one of the last empty chairs. Fiona watched as Paige rose from it now and addressed the committee.

"Good morning, ladies and gentleman." Her voice was strong and authoritative and it caught Fiona a little off guard to see laid-back Paige in a professional capacity. She wondered what Paige was like in her regular life back home. "I'm pleased to announce that I've found a headline act for the program. Miss Veronica Chen, a violinist with the Bay Area Symphony Orchestra, has agreed to perform."

A grumbling sort of murmur filled the room, and it was clear to Fiona that the crowd was a little underwhelmed. *Well, she's not exactly Taylor Swift, now is she?* Fiona indulged in a wicked moment of satisfaction at Veronica's expense, knowing that if her own name had been announced just now, the reaction would have been very different.

Almost as if they'd come to that conclusion in the exact same moment, Liam and half a dozen other members of the Hart family sent pointed glances in her direction. Given the uneasiness that had existed between her and the family since Alice's death, they'd never actually asked for her to participate, but it was clear by their accusing expressions that they were more than a little put out by the fact that she hadn't come around and begged to join in of her own accord. Having sworn off performances entirely to the dismay of venues around the world, Fiona hadn't felt the need to explain herself further in this instance, but as her stomach clenched under their scrutiny, Fiona wondered if that had been a mistake.

A five-minute break was announced, and almost immediately Fiona found Liam beside her.

"Oh, so now you're interested in the music festival, are you?" Liam's voice was gruff.

Fiona sighed. Definitely a miscalculation. She should have dealt with this months before. "It's not that I wasn't interested, Liam. It was just too hard to get involved. It was too soon."

"Too soon? But it's not too soon for you to be seeing someone new? Yes, Fiona, I've figured out your little secret. It was obvious the minute you walked in that you're fucking that American girl."

Fiona gaped, completely taken aback by his crudeness. "Liam Hart, that's none of your business!" She clenched her fists. It's not like she could deny the truth of it, but he made it sound so tawdry. Even if she knew that's what everyone had been thinking.

Liam sniffed, unapologetic. "So why are you here, Fiona?"

"This is my home, Liam." Her words were clipped with anger. "I wanted to get more involved in the community."

"Too bad you didn't feel like that when Alice was alive and could have appreciated it."

Her blood was boiling and she wanted to respond,

but deep down she knew he spoke the truth. Instead she stared straight ahead, seeing red.

"Oh, I get it now. You're not here for Alice at all. You're here to see what you can do to boost that failing business of yours. You don't care about Alice. You couldn't commit to her when she was alive, and you won't even sing for her now that she's dead!"

Liam's volume had steadily increased along with the vitriol of his words. Half the room had heard him by the time he landed that final gut punch. Fiona felt all of their eyes upon her, boring into her, reminding her of what a terrible girlfriend she'd been. She'd let Alice down in her final breath, and everyone here had been a witness. With tears pricking her eyes, she ran from the church and into the stone maze of the churchyard, desperate to escape their silent judgment.

THE VICAR HAD JUST CALLED for a five-minute break when Paige found herself cornered by Harry, the red-headed farmer who'd been so adamant in the previous meeting about getting a famous performer for the festival. Before he had the chance to open his mustached mouth, Paige knew that her efforts to secure Veronica had fallen short of the mark in his estimation.

"Miss Ridley, if I may have a word?"

Paige forced a smile. "Yes, of course."

"I couldn't help but notice that this musician you've engaged for the festival, well, that she's not exactly a household name. Virginia was it?"

"Veronica. And I understand your concerns, I really do, but with so little time to plan, the options are somewhat limited. And she's relatively well-known within classical music circles."

Harry nodded, still looking less than pleased. "Of course. And I'm sure we'll be able to sell a few more tickets because of it. It's just," he hesitated, glancing toward the back of the room where Fiona was engaged in conversation with Liam, "I happened to see you walk in with Miss Blake this morning, and…well, you looked quite friendly together. I'm sure you know her relation to Alice Hart, and about her previous career as a—"

Harry cut his thought short as an outburst from Liam reverberated through the room. Paige froze, uncertain what he'd said, but registering the look of shock and pain on Fiona's face with clarity. As the crowd stared, Fiona turned and ran from the room.

"I'm sorry, Harry. If you'll excuse me."

Without further explanation, Paige followed Fiona out the door and into the hall just in time to see Fiona slip out a door at the far end that led to the outside. Paige ran down the hall and pushed the door open, stepping out into a sea of headstones. She opened her mouth to call out, but closed it again as she saw Fiona stop beside a stone of fresh white marble and sink to her knees with a sob.

Alice's grave. With a sinking heart, Paige realized the truth. As wonderful as the last week with Fiona had been, as often as Paige's thoughts had started to turn to ways to continue to see Fiona when her trip was over, she would be foolish to think that Fiona was ready for that. Tears welled in her own eyes as she regarded the heartbroken woman she'd come to have such strong feelings for. It hit her like a physical blow to see her in such despair.

Paige took a few steps forward, hesitantly. Would Fiona want her to be there? Even though it crushed her to admit that she was no substitute for Fiona's beloved Alice, it was clear that Fiona needed comfort, and Paige loved her too much to let her hurt alone. She continued on her path toward the snowy white stone.

"Fee?" Paige fought to keep her voice steady. "Are you okay? You can talk to me."

"It's nothing." Fiona was curled in a ball on the ground, her head tucked into her arms.

"It isn't nothing. You're sobbing on your dead girlfriend's grave. That's the opposite of nothing." She hoped it didn't sound too harsh, but she needed to cut through Fiona's grief.

She straightened up and looked at Paige. "It was just a disagreement with Liam."

Inwardly, Paige cursed the tactless man for hurting

Fiona like this. He'd obviously been pressuring her to change her mind about performing in his festival. *Why couldn't these people just understand that everyone grieves in their own way, and leave Fee alone!* "I understand how you feel, Fee. I really do. They're all pressuring you to perform. They don't know how much that would take out of you. It's okay for you to say no. You have no reason to feel guilty."

A desperate laugh issued from Fiona's throat, causing Paige's breath to catch. It was an unexpected response, and even more troubling than her tears. "If only that were true!" Fiona closed her eyes, looking beat. "I appreciate your loyalty, Paige, but you don't know the whole story. Liam's issue with me has nothing to do with the music festival."

Paige frowned and knelt down beside Fiona on the cold ground. "Then tell me. What is it?"

Fiona sighed. "It's a long story, but I guess it really boils down to the land."

"Your farm?"

She nodded. "It's been in the Hart family for generations. Liam tried to buy it from Alice's father several years ago, but he wouldn't sell. Her father was a big, stubborn Yorkshire man, and he loved his land. When he died of a heart attack, very sudden, about a year after Alice and I got together, she inherited it all. She was determined for us to fix everything up and run it together, which I'm sure frustrated Liam to no end, but what could he say? She was his cousin, and she had every right to it as a member of the Hart family. What I didn't know until after she died was that she'd left it all to me. It came as a shock to us all."

"So Liam wanted the farm?"

"He did, and does. I think he expected she'd leave it to him with a stipulation that he'd need to buy out my share of the money I'd helped invest in it. That's what I'd thought, too. But when we realized that wasn't the case, he offered to buy it. A generous offer, too."

"But you turned it down?" Paige still wasn't certain how a dispute over land had led to so much emotional turmoil.

"Maybe it was a bad choice." Regret etched fine lines across Fiona's face. "The land's worth a lot more money than you might assume, much more than I could possibly earn from it, and Liam would pay a fair price. Daniel and I would be set. I don't know why I couldn't. It's not like this land is in my blood like it is theirs."

"It doesn't have to be for you to love it. You can fall in love in a heartbeat." Their eyes locked and Paige's heart skipped a beat as she realized what she'd said. *I'm really wearing my heart on my sleeve with that one.* "I'm sorry Fiona. I shouldn't have said that. I know you're not wanting to hear something like that from me. Especially not right now." She rose swiftly to her feet. "I should go."

Fiona stood as well, and grasped Paige's arm,

gently but firmly. "Paige, no! Don't go, and don't apologize. I don't think I've explained this right."

"It's okay. You know whatever it is that happened with it all, you feel guilty. You don't need to."

Fiona winced as if in pain. "But I do, Paige. I *do* need to feel guilty. When Alice got sick, I wasn't even here!"

"But that wasn't your fault. You said yourself that it happened fast."

"But it was hardly the first time I'd been gone. And Paige, by the time I got home, she was already in a coma. She didn't even know I'd returned."

Sadness stabbed Paige's heart at the revelation. *No wonder Fiona's so racked with guilt!* "Fiona, you can't blame yourself. You did everything you could. You loved her. You would have spent the rest of your life with her if you could have. It's just not how it worked out, but that's not your fault."

"The rest of my life…" Fiona half laughed, half gasped as the tears glistened in her eyes. "I'm glad you're certain of that, because I'm not."

A shock of cold passed through Paige's core. "I don't understand. What are you saying?"

"Do you know how many times I thought about proposing? I even had a ring, a family heirloom. But I didn't."

The feeling of coldness lingered, but she tried once more, desperation setting in. "You were just waiting for the right time?"

"Or maybe I was waiting because I wasn't certain," Fiona answered, her voice hardly above a whisper. "Maybe I wasn't certain, deep down, that Alice was right for me. I loved her, but the farm, the pub? It was too much. I wasn't sure I was ready for it."

Fiona gestured around her with her hands as she spoke, and all Paige could see was Veronica, standing in their kitchen, and doing and saying exactly the same thing. *Too much. Not ready.* "So you were just stringing Alice along, until something better turned up?" Paige's voice trembled with raw anger, on her own behalf as well as poor, dead Alice, with whom she felt a sudden, deep bond. *We both know what it's like to be used and deceived by the woman we love.* How was the way Fiona had treated Alice any different from how Veronica had treated Paige?

Fiona looked at Paige in apparent shock. "No, Paige, that's not it. But when I think about what I had with Alice and compare it to the time I've spent with you, I'm not sure I was wrong."

That wasn't what Paige wanted to hear, not in the least. What did it even mean? If she had turned up in Holme and Alice had still been alive, would Fiona have dumped Alice the same way Veronica had dumped her? *After what I went through with Veronica for so long, how did I trust her so quickly? How did I not see this coming?*

"I need to go." With that, Paige started to walk away.

"Hold on, Paige. Wait! Let's talk about this."

Fiona's voice was filled with desperation, but Paige hardened her heart against it.

She shook her head violently back and forth, her head a purple blur. "I don't think so. Not right now."

"At least let me get the car and drive you home," Fiona pleaded.

At the thought of spending another minute in Fiona's company, Paige could feel her skin crawl. "No. I think I could use the walk."

She weaved her way through the stones and out the squeaky gate without a backward glance, pretending her heart wasn't breaking at the sound of Fiona's tears.

FIFTEEN

IT WAS SO quiet in the Black Fleece that afternoon that Fiona could hear the guy at the other end of the bar sipping his beer. The slurping wetness of the sound grated on her. Her spirits plummeted in the oppressive silence and all she could do was assume the worst. Half the village had been in the meeting that day, and everyone of them had heard what Liam had said. He'd accused her of using the meeting for her own gain, a desperate attempt to prop up a failing business. Would any of her neighbors truly disagree?

Why would they? They hate me. I'll lose my business and have to sell the farm to Liam for a fraction of the property's value.

At her lowest point, Fiona sometimes experienced a perverse enjoyment of her own emotional pain. She needed to wallow in it, and this was something she recognized in herself but felt powerless to stop. It's what she had done the past year, and the reason Daniel had fled to the states. Just as she'd come close to exhausting her pain over Alice, she'd stumbled on a new source. *Paige.*

Paige, with her talent and enthusiasm, could have helped her save this place. Look how much she had already accomplished with barely any effort! *But Paige hates me, too.*

Fiona closed her eyes and could see the revulsion on Paige's face at her confession. She'd been foolish to think she wouldn't ruin things with Paige. Fiona couldn't help being a disappointment to the people she loved. *Alice. Daniel. Paige.*

She had the remnants of a beer in front of her, but she craved something stronger. *Not a good idea.* There was wallowing, and then there was crossing a line. There'd been points, maybe more than she cared to admit, in the past year where she'd crossed a line, and she didn't want to do it again. *And yet, there's a new bottle of Jameson on the top shelf.* She licked her parched lips and could feel the desire for it grow. *I need to call Daniel.* She grabbed her phone from her pocket and dialed, but there was no answer.

The last of the patrons departed and Fiona was left alone in the pub. She eyed the familiar silhouette of the bottle, torn. *What does it matter?* She'd become used to the ache of missing Alice, of failing her. But the pain of driving Paige away was raw and angry. It needed soothing. With a surreptitious glance, she stood to fetch it.

A whimper came from the hearth and Fiona froze, steeped in the guilt of her weakness being discovered, even if it was only by her dog. Maxine whined as she stretched her back, then padded over to nuzzle her face against Fiona's shins. With a scratch beneath the chin, Maxie's tail thudded with glee, and a glimmer of hope lit up the darkness of the moment.

"You're right, Maxie. What was I thinking?" She sat on the bar stool again, the craving gone. Maxine gave a yip and rubbed her wet nose against Fiona's hand in approval. She was strong enough to handle this on her own, without a drink, and without leaning on Daniel. She'd just needed to remember it.

With a blast of frigid air, the front door opened and she heard someone call out her name in greeting. Fiona turned to see several regulars settling into their favorite table. A few minutes later, a trio of musicians arrived and start setting up. Over the thirty minutes that Fiona took to nurse her one pint of beer, the pub went from a lifeless void to being loud and hopping.

Fiona lowered her chin and looked into her dog's eyes with chagrin. "You're right. The sky's not falling after all."

It was a reminder she'd needed repeatedly since the phone call in Sydney, when her life had spun out of control. Not every bump in the road was fatal, not every setback was permanent. With a clearer head, she played the conversation with Paige in the graveyard over again in her mind. She hadn't explained herself well, and had been self-indulgent in her wallowing. Knowing what she did about Paige's previous relationship, how she'd been strung along and then heartlessly dumped, it was no wonder her words had struck an unpleasant chord.

But deep down, no matter how much Fiona sometimes wanted to pile blame on herself over the last days of Alice's life, she wasn't like Veronica. She'd had doubts, but not unreasonable ones, and not insurmountable ones. The truth was, she'd loved Alice. She'd moved to the farm for her, put her career on hold for her, and put every penny of her winnings into the land even after Alice was gone. If she'd been given the chance, she would have married her and spent her life with her. And they would have been happy enough.

Paige never would have come to Holme, and I would never have known what it felt like to meet that once-in-a-lifetime person, that person who fits like no other, because I never would have met Paige. Guilt squeezed Fiona's insides. The last thing she wanted was to dismiss Alice's importance, and she knew that's how it would sound if she said it out loud. She wished she knew the secret to honoring what she'd lost and rejoicing in what she'd found in equal measure. But even more important now that she'd found her was not to lose Paige again.

Sliding her empty pint glass away from her, on the bar, Fiona's fists clenched and she rose to leave.

Maxine trotted along at her side into the evening's bitter wind. Her coat was wrapped tightly across her chest, held fast by cold fingers, as she climbed the hill to the cottage. She pictured the soft, welcoming glow of the porch light, and her stride lengthened. She wasn't sure what she'd say when she got there, but somehow she'd make Paige understand that it had all been an unfortunate misunderstanding.

But when she arrived at the cottage, the porch remained dark, and no lamplight shone through the windows. There wasn't a single sign of life, even though Paige should have arrived home hours ago. As she fretted, the wind tore at her exposed cheeks, and Fiona's heart clenched as she pictured Paige walking home alone. *What if something happened to her?* Fiona's pulse thudded in her ears. *What if she'd taken a shortcut through a field and got lost?*

Frantically, Fiona turned her head, scanning for some sign of Paige that she'd overlooked, when it finally registered that Daniel's car was gone. Paige must have taken it for a drive, but where? Dejected, she realized that it wasn't any of her business where Paige had gone. At least she knew she'd made it home safely, which offered some small consolation.

Fiona sighed, the air turning her breath to ice on her lips. She couldn't exactly stand out all night until Paige came home. Their conversation might need to wait until morning. Her back straightened, resolute. She would use the delay to figure out what to say; to plan her attack. The one certainty was that she couldn't lose her. She couldn't let Paige go over a misunderstanding. She needed to explain. She needed to fight for her.

WHEN SHE'D STORMED out of the graveyard, Paige had been so riled up she was impervious to the cold. Half a mile into her walk, this was no longer the case. She stamped her feet on the ground as she walked to keep the blood flowing. She blew on her bare fingertips and stuffed them deep into her pockets for warmth. All the while, she fought back tears.

It was time to face facts. This whole trip had been a bust. Instead of relaxing and contemplating her life goals, she'd volunteered herself to head up a music festival. The film score she'd been set to write, though she'd finally had some ideas, still lacked even a single note written on paper. And the ex-girlfriend she was supposed to be getting thousands of miles away from? *Yeah, even that got screwed up.* She yanked her phone from her pocket, ignoring the protest of her frozen fingers, and pulled up a familiar number. There was only one way to fix the mess she'd made.

"Brittany? It's Paige." She drew a breath to continue, but stopped, perplexed, as she realized her friend's voice was just a recording. She bit her lip as she waited for the beep. "Brit? It's me. I need to come home. Call me back, okay?"

A surge of annoyance got her heart pounding faster, warming her more than mere exercise had done. *Where is she?* Brittany always answered the phone, even when she was at work. It was a work day, wasn't it? Paige realized with a start that she'd kind of lost track, but she thought it was. Maybe the governor's office was holding a press conference.

The phone rang.

"Paige?" Her friend sounded out of breath, like she'd been exercising. Paige frowned, wondering when Brittany had started going to the gym. *"What's this about coming home?"* Brittany's voice was stern and scolding. There was a low murmuring in the background.

"Oh, Brit. I screwed everything up, and I'm not getting any work done here, anyway. And I just want to come home." Paige was desperate to cry, but now that she was finally willing to let them flow, the tears remained stubbornly in place. Bitterly, she wondered if they'd frozen in their ducts.

"Sorry, Paige, but that's really not going to work right now." Paige listened in shocked silence as her best friend refused to help her. It had never happened before. There was a shuffling, crinkling sound coming over the phone, and she thought she heard Brittany's voice whisper 'just another minute,' followed by a murmur and some giggling. *Giggling?*

"What do you mean it's not going to work?"

"I mean that I'm…" That was definitely giggling, followed by a louder 'stop that' that didn't sound at all sincere to Paige's ear. *"Paige, it's not a good time."*

At last, the clues clicked into place. Brittany was *not* alone. "Where are you right now? It doesn't sound like you're at work." She hoped more than ever that she was right about it being a workday, because she was going to feel really foolish if it wasn't.

"No, I took some vacation time. I'm at home." And then a scolding 'Danny, be patient…' echoed in Paige's ear. *Danny? Surely not Fiona's* brother *Danny?*

"Brit, what's going on? You never take vacation."

There was an exasperated sigh. *"If you must know, Daniel and I are, well, having a thing."*

"A thing?"

"A thing, Paige. A naked thing. Do I need to spell it out?"

Paige cringed. "No, I think I've got a visual. When you say Daniel, you mean Daniel whose cottage I'm staying in right now?"

"Yes, that's the one. I told you he was my type. That's the good news, right? The bad news is that there's no way we want you as a third wheel right now. But more good news! You can stay in the cottage longer if you'd like."

"Great." She stabbed the end call button with an icy appendage.

How could Brittany do this? She was a workaholic. She wasn't supposed to start having a love life right when Paige needed her! Guilt needled her, but Paige dismissed it as the cold starting to freeze her insides as much as her exterior. With the village outlined ahead, she increased her pace.

Her feet stomped furiously, and it was no use pretending it was due to the cold. She knew she was being selfish, but she didn't care. Reaching her cottage door, Paige threw open the door, then slammed it with a satisfying thud and threw herself into a chair. *I just need to feel like someone wants me right now. Is that so much to ask?*

As if on cue, her phone rang. Paige smiled triumphantly at Brittany's change of heart, and answered the phone without so much as a glance at the screen. "Calling to say you're sorry?" she asked saucily.

"Um, Paige?"

With a sharp intake of breath, Paige realized she'd made a mistake. "Veronica?"

"What's that about apologizing?"

Paige groaned. "Never mind. I thought you were someone else." Veronica was one person who would never say she was sorry about anything.

"Oh, well that's a relief. Look, I'm passing through West Yorkshire and thought we could have dinner."

"Yeah, fine." Paige answered from reflex, her brain so muddled from the fight with Fiona and the sting of Brittany's rejection that the words were out before she'd remembered who she was talking to. This was Veronica! She might be craving attention, but God knows Veronica was hardly the best place to get it. *And yet…the timing's a bit too perfect*. How bad would it really be just to meet for a friendly dinner?

"I'll meet you in an hour."

Before disappointment in herself overwhelmed her, Paige reminded herself that they needed to discuss the festival. *It's just business.* It had nothing to do with Fiona, not that she would care, anyway, what Paige did. *Two peas in a pod, Veronica and Fiona*. She would be better off without either one of them.

Glaring at the car Daniel had left for her use, and trying with all her strength not to remember what Daniel and her best friend were currently getting up to back home, Paige plunked herself onto the seat. Then she realized there was no steering wheel in front of her, screamed at the top of her lungs for a full thirty seconds, and tried again on the other side.

Thankfully, she made it to the restaurant without further incident, and when she entered she saw Veronica waiting for her at a table near the window.

"Veronica, it's nice to see you again." She extended her right hand for a business-like handshake and was sucked into a full body hug instead.

"Oh, Paige, I've missed you!" Veronica pressed a kiss to her cheek. Her lips lingered so long Paige worried they'd gotten stuck. "I've been thinking about you so much since Harrogate. You look beautiful, by the way."

"You do, too," she fumbled in reply as the heat

rushed to her face at the compliment. *Damn it, Paige, get your act together!* She was supposed to be here to conduct business, not to blush like a schoolgirl.

Veronica sighed an exaggerated Veronica-like sigh. "Sometimes I wonder what I was thinking last year."

Paige's brow wrinkled as she tried to process what she'd just heard. It had almost been an apology. If she didn't know any better, she might think Veronica wanted her back. Oddly, the prospect of a contrite Veronica made her wary. She'd never seen this side of her before, which made her unpredictable. *Is she sincere?* But maybe she was being too cautious and needed to give her a chance?

No. She's had enough chances.

She struggled to get the meeting back on track. "So, regarding the festival format—"

"Maybe when you're back in the Bay area, we can get together?"

"Veronica..." She'd be lying to say she wasn't tempted. Veronica was on her best behavior tonight. Charming, flirtatious. And she was still so wounded from the fight with Fiona in the graveyard. Every inch of Paige was an exposed nerve. But as she looked across the table at her ex's expectant face, it wasn't the face she wanted to see. Throat constricting, she forced out her reply. "I don't think that's a good idea."

Her stomach fluttered, but it was the only choice. Whatever else happened, Paige understood that, no matter what Veronica seemed to be offering, Paige deserved better than what Veronica would ultimately give. And while it was likely that things were over between her and Fiona after today, until they were resolved, there was no way that Paige could move on.

Veronica shrugged. "Well, it was worth a try." Her voice had a sing-song quality to it, like a woman who asked a question but didn't really care one way or the other what the answer was. "Oh, by the way, about that festival on Christmas Eve?" Paige's pulse quickened as if she already knew instinctively what was coming. "I'm afraid I'm going to have to give it a pass."

Anger bubbled to her surface. "What? But I've already told everyone you were doing it."

"I'm sorry Paige-y. I said I was fairly certain I could do it. But it turns out I can't. There's somewhere else I need to be. There you go, not listening to me again, just like always."

That she was certain that wasn't what Veronica had said was neither here nor there. Like every time this had happened in the past, she would have to agree to disagree in order to move on. Veronica would never admit to being wrong. And the truth was that sometimes Paige *had* heard what she wanted to hear. Sometimes she'd jumped to conclusions without getting all the details. It's not what she'd done with the festival, but she realized with a sinking heart that it may have happened somewhere else that day. *Is that what I did to Fiona?*

She'd accused Fiona of being like Veronica, but with the real thing sitting across from her in the flesh, Paige reconsidered. Could she really imagine Fiona behaving like this, tearing through her life with all the care and compassion of a category four hurricane? It was impossible to visualize. And now that she thought about it, she couldn't believe that Fiona had treated Alice that way, either. It's not something she would do. This all had to be a misunderstanding, and she could have sorted it out if only she'd stayed long enough to hear Fiona out.

"Paige-y, are listening to me?"

Paige stared at Veronica. For the first time she felt that she was seeing her for what she had always been. It was illuminating, and heart wrenching, and it made her feel slightly sick to have been a fool for so long. "No, Veronica, I'm not. And if you'll excuse me, I need to go. There's somewhere else I'm supposed to be."

SIXTEEN

THE ARCTIC COLD snap had not improved with the sunrise. Fiona could attest to this first hand, because she'd watched it come up while walking the perimeter of the property to check for broken fences. Even in the winter, sheep needed to go out, a fact that had never occurred to her in her pre-farm days. Though Brandon would give them their hay in the barn in cold weather, the doors were left wide open so the sheep could come and go as they pleased throughout the day. It was almost like they enjoyed being outside in temperatures like this. *Stupid little buggers.* All Fiona wanted was to stay inside from Christmas until late spring at the earliest. *A mug of hot tea, a roaring fire, some thick wool socks...*

Though as long as she was making her Christmas wish list, what she really wanted was to be back in Paige's good graces. Was that something Father

Christmas could deliver on his sleigh? Could he make it an early delivery while he was at it? Christmas Eve was almost two weeks away, and she'd rather not have to wait. There wouldn't be much time after that before Paige went away, and Fiona wanted as many days together as possible. She knew better than to ask Father Christmas for a more permanent arrangement. She'd been much too naughty for that.

No, not naughty. She'd punished herself as if she had been, but what had she done, really, except make what had seemed like reasonable choices at the time? Investing in her singing career, going to Sydney to compete? None of those were bad decisions by themselves. She'd poured her energy into her voice the way Alice had poured hers into the farm, and for the same reasons. She'd just wanted a comfortable, happy life with the woman she loved, and she'd gone about achieving it in the best way she knew how. She'd had no way of knowing what was to come when she boarded the plane to Australia, and yet she'd punished herself for the past year as if she had.

She'd abandoned her music, forced herself to stay on the farm, and given up on everything that mattered to her. She'd allowed herself to lean too heavily on her brother, even when she knew that doing so was driving him away. And every day she'd blamed herself for failing Alice, from the moment she awoke until the end of the day, until it was the only thing left that defined her. It was no wonder the description she'd given of herself had led Paige to think she was a monster. She'd thought so herself, until Paige had come into her life and helped her see everything through fresh eyes.

At the corner of the property, Fiona paused and looked out across the land. *Her land*. She'd cared for the farm as a duty she owed to Alice's memory, some way of making up for not being there to take care of her. But she hadn't appreciated the beauty of what she had until Paige arrived and showed her the potential that surrounded her. A failing pub could become a thriving piano bar. A neighborhood of strangers might become a community. Even an old Christmas song could transform into something new. All it took was some inspiration.

She continued her walk as Maxine, once a morose little creature who hung out in graveyards, bounded around her like a puppy again. Fiona's laughter jingled like a sleigh bell. *She's even improved my dog!* That's why it was so important to hold onto Paige as long as she could. It might not be forever, but Fiona knew that each day with Paige contained a magic that would linger long after she'd gone. It's why she needed to patch things up between them as quickly as she could. If only she knew how.

Lost in thought, Fiona drifted through the pasture home, until Maxine's growl broke the silence. Fiona's stomach clenched when she saw the cause of the dog's distress. There was Dolly, standing at the wall. And on the other side was Paige. *If I'm going to do this, there's no time like the present...* Willing herself to remain courageous, she squared her shoulders and approached, hoping the words would come to her.

"Paige, I've been—" She managed only three words before Paige broke in.

"I was an idiot, Fee." Hardly the response she'd been expecting.

"No, I was the idiot!"

"No," Paige was adamant. "It was definitely me."

On the verge of affirming her idiocy once more, Fiona's voice of reason interrupted. *Maybe you could try not being an idiot long enough to put an end to this idiotic argument?* "Let's agree that neither of us was at her best yesterday, shall we?"

Paige nodded. "Things were going so well that I was certain something was going to mess us up. I was literally waiting for it to happen. And sometimes I have a tendency to hear what I expect to hear instead of what's being said. I didn't give you a chance to explain."

"And I was being self-indulgent and melodramatic and never once stopped to think what it would sound like to someone other than myself." She reached out a gloved hand and placed it over Paige's where it rested on the stone wall. "There have been so many times that you've just seemed to know what I meant to say, even when I didn't say it right, that I've become spoiled."

Paige lowered her gaze shyly. "And I forgot how important it is to communicate instead of running away. I'm sorry."

"I am, too." Fiona squeezed Paige's hand.

Paige laughed. "It took about two seconds of being around Veronica last night to realize that you would *never* treat someone the way she does."

"You saw Veronica?" Wariness flooded her at the mention of Veronica's name.

Paige let out a long breath, as if to emphasize how laborious the experience had been. "I did. And you won't believe it, but she can't do the festival after all."

"What? But she promised! She even told some of the people at the Christmas party about it."

"I knew I wasn't imagining it!" Paige's eyes narrowed. "God, no wonder I don't know what I've heard half the time. Veronica says one thing and denies it in the next breath. I regret ever being with her!"

Fiona's relief was almost tangible, but a nagging worry tugged at her. "Paige, you know that I won't ever regret the years I spent with Alice. I loved her, and I would have married her if we'd been given that chance."

"Good. I'm glad." The sincerity of her smile made Fiona's heart sing.

Speaking of singing… "So, what are you going to do about the festival?"

"Oh, I'm basically screwed. There's no way I can

find another headline act with only two weeks to go. I'll have to tell the committee." Though she tried to make light of it, Fiona could see the disappointment in her eyes.

Fiona trembled. The solution was obvious, but could she do it? Paige would never ask. She'd have to offer, if only she knew for certain that she was ready. For a second time that morning, her voice of reason broke through the muddle in her head. *If you want her to understand how you feel, you have to take a chance.*

"I have a better idea." Fiona paused, wanting to make certain Paige really understood what she was about to say. "Tell them I'm doing it."

"You don't have to do that!"

"I want to." With a start, she realized that it was true. She'd been afraid before, but already she could feel the thrill of performing building inside. The fact that Paige would instinctively know how she felt only intensified it. "Paige, you need to understand something. This is really important. I'm not offering because of Alice. It's just for you." She'd feared she wouldn't know what to say before, but now the words flowed so fast she couldn't stop them. "I'm doing it because you've helped me to enjoy life again, and because I know how much this means to you, and because I think…I think I'm falling in love with you."

"You think so?" Paige's eyes were wide.

"Yes. I think so." Fiona waited, breathless, for a response but Paige remained quiet for so long she couldn't take it anymore. "Well, aren't you going to say anything in return?"

"I already did. Yesterday. Remember, when we were in the cemetery?"

Fiona pouted as she tried to recall. "I'm sure I would remember. Could I have been so wrapped up in my own suffering that I just didn't hear?"

"Perhaps it was just implied. But just so we're singing from the same hymn sheet as you say here…I love you. And given that I'm only here another three weeks, and I live eight thousand miles away, it's safe to say that there's no *thinking* involved in any of this. But I can't help it. I do."

Fiona leaned across the wall the separated them and claimed Paige's mouth with her lips. An instant heat flared up between them, but soon the feel of Paige's frozen nose against her face reminded her of the frigid weather. "It's freezing out here! Maybe we should go inside and warm up?"

A sly smile teased Paige's lips. "It's *really* cold. It might take a very, *very* long time to warm up."

Fiona grinned as she bounded over the low stone wall, so full of life that she saw no reason to bother with the gate. "I don't have any other plans today, do you?"

"Not a single one." Paige leaned against her, nudging her toward the cottage path with her shoulder. "And I'm free all evening, too."

PAIGE AWOKE EARLY the next morning, a song echoing so loudly in her mind that it wouldn't let her rest. It was the melody she'd created with Fiona, the one that would be turned into a score for Mike's film. It had bubbled and brewed on the back burner of her consciousness long enough, and now demanded her immediate attention. With a regretful glance at the still-sleeping Fiona, snuggled so comfortably in her bed, Paige considered lingering but knew it was no use. Inspiration called, and she knew that was something Fiona would understand. With a scribbled note left on the pillow, she headed to the Black Fleece to work out some of her ideas on the piano in the quiet hours before the place opened for lunch.

It was just after eleven o'clock when the first customers began to file in. Setting aside her work and emerging from a creative fog, Paige noted with a start that Harry had entered the pub and was walking her way.

"Morning, Harry! Did you get my message about Fiona singing for the festival?"

He let out a hearty chuckle. "Did I ever! The announcement was sent out yesterday afternoon and we're nearly sold out."

Pride swelled her chest. "That's amazing! How many tickets are left?"

He considered a moment. "Twenty-five, although

we could probably squeeze in some folding chairs along the aisles, and make it fifty. That extra £2500 would be nice. Only problem is, all the hotels in the area are sold out. We might have some luck in Huddersfield, but it's a bit of a drive. I'm just on my way to see about setting up transportation."

Paige nodded in sympathy. "No room at the inn. You can't have a more Christmas-y problem than that, can you?"

Harry's forehead crinkled, then he laughed appreciatively as he caught on to the joke. "No, indeed! Perhaps I should look into getting people rooms in a local barn, in keeping with the holiday spirit."

"Agritourism's all the rage now, Harry. You just might get some takers!" A forgotten detail danced at the edge of Paige's memory. "The inn…Hey, Harry, you've lived here a long time. Didn't the Black Fleece used to be some kind of an inn?"

He nodded. "It was, back when Alice's father ran the place. But it's been a while."

Paige's brain whirled. "Okay, I can't promise anything, but I just had an idea. Let me talk to Fiona and see if there's any way the rooms upstairs could be used for this. I'm not sure it would hold fifty, but maybe half that."

"Well, £1250 would still go a long way for the charity."

As Harry departed, the figure he'd mentioned ran through her head in a loop. She frowned. £50 per ticket? It sounded a lot higher than the figures she remembered from the packet Liam had given her. She could have sworn the charity had estimated earning only £25 per ticket, but maybe she was mistaken.

"Hello, my early bird!" Fiona had sneaked up behind her as Paige was deep in thought. Her soft greeting tickled Paige's ear and sent all thoughts of facts and figures far away. "Did you get some work done?"

Paige nodded and showed her the stack of music sheets beside her that were covered in penciled notes. Though pleased at what she'd accomplished, the sound of Fiona's voice was the most beautiful music she'd heard all day.

"Apparently you still have a few fans out there." Paige smiled at Fiona's confused expression. "I just talked to Harry. Tickets have almost sold out since we announced you were joining the show."

"Well, flattering as that would be, it's not just word of mouth from fans. I told Philip about the show, and you can imagine how eager he was to get the word out. We have him to thank, though I may live to regret it when he calls in the favor."

"There's just one problem. The hotels in the valley are all booked, and some people are still looking for a place to stay. So I was thinking, what about here?"

"Here? How could they stay here?"

"You said you have guest rooms upstairs," Paige reminded her, warming even more to the idea. "I know they haven't been used in a while, but how bad could they be?"

"I hate to say it, but I honestly don't know. That was Alice's department. But as the owner, I suppose that's my job now." She held out her hand to Paige. "Shall we go see?"

There was a set of stairs off a back room that Paige hadn't even known existed. They were hidden from view in the main part of the pub, and the entrance that serviced them was never used. As they climbed to the second floor, Paige grew giddy. Aside from her music, there was nothing she enjoyed more than a good fixer-upper project. Brittany had nearly lost the use of her television over the past year to Paige's obsessive watching of home improvement shows.

At the top of the stairs was a large sitting room with a fireplace, which Paige was relieved to see had been left clean and in appeared to be in good repair. She counted fifteen rooms in all, each with an assortment of old-fashioned furniture in various states of repair. None of the pieces were quite nice enough to be called antique, but with a coat of paint and some stenciling, Paige thought they could be transformed into something approaching shabby country chic. There were mattresses in decent condition, though there were no sheets or other linens, and no decor of any kind.

Paige studied the walls closely. "Is this a fresh coat of paint?"

Fiona nodded. "Alice had the whole place painted right after we took over, including up here. She envisioned remodeling the rooms in a sleek, modern style, but we could never afford to do more than the paint."

"Do you have any money to spend on it now?"

"A little in savings that I could spare. Not much, though."

"I wouldn't need much. With only two weeks to do it, I'll have to work with what's here, but it would be helpful if there's enough for new linens and curtains, and some decorations. It won't be sleek and modern, but I think we can pull off country cozy."

"In two weeks?" Fiona looked shocked. "Are you sure? It looks like a wreck to me."

"Sure." Paige gave a confident shrug. "Some faux finishes, a few decorative knick-knacks here and there, and the guests will love it.

Fiona shook her head, bewildered. "I have no idea what you're talking about, but I guess I'll trust you to know what needs to be done."

"Can I get Brandon and some of his men to help move the furniture?"

"You're the boss! Actually, Maria's more the boss when it comes to Brandon. Let's go down and check with her about his schedule."

As they walked into the kitchen, Maria handed Paige a spoon. "Here, stir this." Paige took it and did as she was told.

Fiona placed her hands on her hips in mock outrage. "Why don't you ever give me a job to do?"

"You burn things."

From her spot at the stove, Paige snorted at Maria's deadpan answer.

Fiona shrugged. "It's true. I really do. So Maria, do you think Paige could borrow Brandon this week to move some furniture upstairs?"

"Upstairs? You mean in the old inn?"

Paige filled Maria in on the plan, and when she'd finished, the cook clapped her hands in delight. "Maybe we can get them to stay for my Christmas dinner. It's still undersold."

Paige's face lit up. "That's brilliant! It would be like a bed and breakfast, only with dinner."

"I could set out sandwiches upstairs in the sitting room for Christmas Eve, make it like a party. You could include it in the price of the room."

"How much do you think we could charge?" Fiona asked.

"A lot!" Paige grinned. "It's not just room and board, you know. They get to have Christmas dinner with a worldwide singing sensation. People would pay through the nose!"

Fiona laughed. "I doubt that."

Paige's expression grew serious. "Don't sell yourself short. You'd be amazed what people are willing to pay. In fact, we should see about sending a last-minute advertisement by email to everyone who's bought tickets already. Come to Christmas dinner with Fiona Blake!" Paige said it like she was reading a headline.

Fiona grew pensive. "If we do this, between the guests and a sold-out dinner, I think we have a chance to end the year in the black."

THE NEXT TWO weeks saw a flurry of activity at the Black Fleece, as paint and supplies were brought in, curtains hung, beds made, and decorations put into place. Paige bought out the contents of a charity shop in Huddersfield, nearly down to their last lamp and vase. With her eye for design, she'd soon transformed the old rooms into a cozy, inviting space worthy of any country-living magazine.

Fiona mostly stayed away while the work was being done, focusing instead on readying her voice for the show. After a year of retirement, she knew she had to be serious about it if she was going to deliver a performance she could feel proud of. They spent their evenings together, eating a late dinner at the Black Fleece then retreating to the farmhouse for the night, but Fiona never ventured upstairs. How Paige spent her days remained mostly a mystery to her until just a few days before Christmas Eve when, after dinner was finished, Paige clasped her hands together and started bouncing up and down in her chair.

"It's ready! Do you wanna come see?"

"What's ready? You mean, upstairs?"

Paige grinned. "Yes! And good thing, since the first guests arrive tomorrow afternoon."

They climbed the stairs, and even before they'd reached the top, Fiona could detect a wafting scent of cinnamon and oranges. They emerged into the sitting room, decked from floor to ceiling in yuletide spirit. A Christmas tree sat in one corner, its white lights sparkling off the multi-colored glass balls dangling from its branches. Logs crackled merrily in the fireplace, where a row of hand-knit stockings hung from the mantle. Groupings of chairs and sofas around the large room were hardly recognizable as the same old, tired pieces that had been there before, piled as they were with a fresh assortment of pillows.

Fiona's jaw dropped. "You did all this in under two weeks?"

Paige giggled. "Wait until you see the rooms!"

No two rooms looked alike, and each was more charming than the next, their mismatched contents pulled together in subtle ways that made it seem that it had all been made to go together from the start. Fiona took it in, silently awed, but a knot started to form inside her stomach. *This had to have cost a fortune.*

"Paige, how much more do I owe you?"

Paige frowned. "What do you mean?"

"I only gave you £5,000. How much more did you need?"

Paige gave her a funny look. "None. I didn't even spend all of what you gave me!"

Fiona stared in disbelief. "How is that possible?"

"Because most of it, I didn't have to buy." She laughed at Fiona's confusion, clearly pleased with herself. "See that trunk over there? Your brother had it in the attic at the cottage, filled with old glass Christmas ornaments. I put the balls on the tree and gave the trunk a good cleaning with some furniture polish. Then I started asking the neighbors."

Fiona's eyes grew wide. "The neighbors? What exactly did you ask them?" The thought of asking her neighbors for anything would never have occurred to her.

Paige shrugged. "I just told them what I was doing and asked if they had anything they wanted to get rid of. You wouldn't believe how grateful some of them were to give me their old junk!"

"Paige, I don't see any old junk."

"Well, I should hope not! See those pillows in the sitting room?" As she pointed, Fiona counted at least three dozen. She wasn't an expert, but she was fairly certain she'd seen ones like them in the shops for £20 a piece. She swallowed roughly as she did the calculations in her head. "Those came from four different neighbors, all beat up and in different prints, of course. I got bargain fabric that was discounted even more because it had a stain running down one end, but we just cut that off. Then I paid one of the local teenage girls £1 a piece to sew them together. The whole thing was maybe £50."

Every room teemed with items that had similar stories. A box of old jars from a barn transformed into vases. Old books on the shelves that someone had been ready to throw away. Framed vintage photos, lace curtains that had been shortened to hide a hole. Somehow, Paige had recognized each one as a treasure.

"And they just gave you all this?" Fiona still felt shaky from the surprise of it all.

"Of course. They wanted to help."

Fiona nodded. "Because of Alice."

"No, Fee. Because of you. They said you were very brave dealing with everything this past year. And they wished they knew you better, and had felt uncertain whether you'd welcome their intrusions, but they've really wanted to help." She rattled off the reasons on her fingers like she was counting from a list. "So, do you like it?"

Tears stung Fiona's eyes. "It's so beautiful, I don't even want to go home." She sniffed and wiped her eyes with the back of her hand. "When I have the money to redo my house, I'm flying you over from America to do it."

It was perfectly silent for a moment, the reality of Paige's upcoming departure weighing heavily on them both.

"I'd like that," Paige replied, her voice quavering.

"Or even if you don't redo it soon…I mean, it's not really so far."

Fiona laced her fingers through Paige's and lifted her hand, pressing it firmly to her lips. "No, it's not really that far at all, is it?"

SEVENTEEN

IT WAS an hour before the concert was set to begin on Christmas Eve, and the church was already packed with people who'd traveled into the valley early to stay ahead of an approaching winter storm. Outside, a light snow had already begun to fall, tiny flakes blanketing the ground in a thin layer of white. The forecast called for more later in the day. Paige rubbed her hands together vigorously, in part to keep them warm and in part to relieve the tension that made her feel like a spring wound too tight.

She eyed the churchyard nervously from her vantage point at one of the side doors. Her experience with snow was limited to the visits she'd made to her grandparents' house at Christmas, or weekend trips to the cabin her parents sometimes rented in the mountains when she was young. Snow was for occasional fun, not something she'd ever had to live with or work in every day. It felt like a lot of the fluffy stuff had fallen already, at least to her untrained eye, and the unknowns of dealing with it caused her some heightened concern. But she was excited, too. She couldn't think of anything that would make it feel more like a real Christmas than awakening to the countryside dressed in sparkling white on Christmas morning!

Paige shook her head again at the realization that Christmas was here already. The days had rushed past, the memory of them a blur, like watching a train race past a station platform without stopping. Guiding her thoughts away from how the rest of her time in Holme would fly by just as fast, she focused instead on the flurry of holiday preparations all around her, and the pleasant hum of anticipation it brought.

When she'd checked in with Maria at the Black Fleece before heading to the church, she'd found that preparations were well underway for dinner the next day. Their last minute marketing had been an unqualified success, and they were expecting nearly two hundred people between the two seatings on Christmas day. Under Maria's direction, the dining area had been spruced up for the occasion, with white tablecloths covering the usually bare wood tables, candles in glass votive holders adorning their centers, and boughs of greenery festooning the walls and doorways. Paige, being busy elsewhere, had not been a part of the efforts and had been surprised and delighted by the result.

A faint smile teased her lips as she remembered her visit to the kitchen. The heavenly smells of ginger and cloves coming from that space had made Paige's mouth water. If she hadn't been so eager to hear Fiona sing, she would have been willing to fast forward immediately to noon the next day. All around her, the kitchen had been a buzzing hive of activity. Maria had hired several local girls to help with the food preparations, with herself as the undisputed queen bee, ordering her staff around with enviable efficiency. With all the work she was doing, it was easy to forget that the cook was in her third trimester, but Paige noticed there were times she had paused to rub her back wearily, or appeared frazzled by the untrained status of a few of her newest recruits. Paige had made a mental note to see if there was something she could help with the next day.

The inn, of course, received the lion's share of her interest. They'd booked fifteen couples into the rooms upstairs, and Paige had been relieved to hear that the guests had all arrived safely. Maria had hired two extra helpers from the village to attend to the needs of the inn. One of them had experience working at a larger hotel in the valley and was acting as the manager, so Paige rested easily knowing that her involvement in the project had ended with the decorating. She hadn't a clue how to run an inn, other than making it look pretty, and Fiona knew even less about it, but Maria had once again proved herself a treasure.

Though it was only a trial run, Paige believed the Black Fleece could function quite lucratively as an inn over time. She'd seen Fiona eying her checkbook nervously and knew the extra labor costs from the inn and dinner seatings had her concerned, but the boost in income would offset most of it, and with a little luck, the operation would earn a modest profit within its first year. So far all the feedback Paige had heard had been positive. The guests had loved the vintage decor, and vowed to recommend the inn to all their friends and post their pictures on social media. Each time she thought about it, Paige glowed.

Paige nibbled her lip as the snow continued to swirl outside, her stomach fluttering relentlessly as more people packed into the church. The irony was not lost on her that she brimmed with confidence when it came to the inn, a subject she knew nothing about, and was on the verge of worrying a hole right through her lower lip over the music festival, a topic on which she was supposed to be an expert. Part of it was that she'd had very little real involvement in the thing. It had been mostly planned before she'd been asked to join, and even though the big day had arrived, she was still a little unclear on what they expected her to do.

As far as she could tell, beyond influencing Fiona to take the lead part, her role was ceremonial at best. She'd given a thumbs-up on the program they'd already designed but other than giving the committee bragging rights for including a *professional* musician from America, she wasn't deluded into thinking that she'd served much of a purpose. She wasn't even performing a song, although frankly, that was a relief. Paige preferred the intimate setting of a smaller crowd, with her ideal venue being something very much like the Black Fleece.

You'd make a great scapegoat if anything goes wrong. The thought was uncharacteristically cynical for her. She quickly pushed it aside, but its influence lurked in the corner of her mind. She knew it wasn't fair, but ever since Fiona's upsetting encounter with Liam at the final planning meeting, Paige's opinion of the man had darkened. There were just certain things that didn't add up, like why, even though the committee had clearly been clamoring for it, he'd never asked Fiona to perform. Or why the numbers on his charity report were significantly lower than the festival income. There were at least a dozen other good reasons, Paige was sure. And seeing as it was Christmas, she vowed to focus on those instead of her own prejudice.

At a cue from one of the sound techs, Paige sat at the soundboard, a pair of headphones covering her ears like ear muffs. There was a professional company running the sound, but because she'd had experience with similar equipment, she'd been asked to help with a series of sound checks to free up one of the guys who was struggling to repair a broken mike. As she waited to be asked to push a button or turn a dial, she heard the muffled sound of two male voices coming through the headphones.

They've left one of the mikes hot, Paige thought, searching the controls to find the culprit. It was one they had situated in an alcove where choir members would be stationed during the final act. She swiveled her head toward the location, and saw the recognizably burly figure of Liam talking to an unknown second man. Just as she was about to take off the headphones and go to switch off the mike, she heard Liam say Fiona's name.

She grasped the headphones, poised to remove them, when she paused to listen.

"...getting her up on stage could be the best outcome. She's sure to want to return to her career full time after this, don't you think?"

I couldn't agree more. Fiona had turned her back on performing for all the wrong reasons. It was in her blood, just as the land had been in Alice's. Getting back to it in some capacity would do wonders for her outlook. Paige smiled, touched that Liam recognized that, too.

Technically, she knew that keeping the headphones on and continuing to listen was eavesdropping, and therefore wrong. She should take them off and set them down as she'd been about to do, but temptation rendered her temporarily incapable of following through.

The other man spoke. "I thought the fence breaks

would do her in, especially after she paid to replace the whole thing and they kept happening."

You're right about that. In the weeks since she'd arrived, there had been two small breaks, and Fiona was at her wits' end over them. Though something in the man's tone set Paige's teeth on edge. *He didn't sound all that upset about it…damn. I'm doing it again.* She shook her head and vowed to be more charitable.

Liam chimed in. "That's what you get for keeping a bloody llama to watch the sheep!"

Their laughter had definitely been mean-spirited that time. Paige stiffened. *Hey, that's Dolly you're talking about!* Paige had grown extremely fond of the fluffy llama and her daily visits to the cottage garden.

"Do llamas really break down fences?" asked the other man.

"Hell if I know." Liam's voice was gruff, and in the forced intimacy of the headphones, it grated on Paige in a way that she hadn't noticed in person. "But it's not like either of them do either, do they?" This time their snickering caused her fists to clench so tightly her knuckles strained white against the skin. The cold snap had left her fingers chapped, and the action sent a dull pain through them that only heightened her annoyance. *Why are they being so nasty all of a sudden?*

"I mean, it's not like I wanted to do it, you know?" Liam continued. "I just wanted her to realize she would be better off selling."

Now Paige's thoughts were churning, fitting

together puzzle pieces like she was Nancy Drew. *Did he just admit to breaking the fences himself?* She drew a sharp breath.

"Well, you wouldn't have had to if Alice hadn't gone and given your family's land to that dark-skinned dyke girlfriend of hers."

The man's hateful words made Paige gasp. *That rat-bastard! How dare he say something like that about Fiona!* She fought an urge to storm over and hit him on the back of the head with a music stand. Given her track record, the vicar would never let her through the doors again if she did. Her one consolation was knowing that even Liam wouldn't stand for someone talking about his beloved cousin and her girlfriend that way.

"You know, Russell," Liam paused, gearing up to speak his mind. "What's funny is that I never would've guessed Alice was into that kind of thing. You know what I mean? She always seemed so normal. And so pretty, too, like all the Hart women are. She could've found a man without a problem. I'll never understand it."

At that moment, Paige experienced a dramatic temperature shift through to her core, but whether she'd frozen solid or was burning with the white heat of rage, it was impossible to discern. She was incapable of thought.

"Well, if you're lucky, Fiona will be back on tour and eager to sell before you know it."

"She'd better not expect full price, though."

After this, the conversation faded, the two men having wandered away from the mike to some other part of the church. As the power of thought and movement slowly returned to her, a tingling overtaking her numb limbs, one goal consumed her. *I need to tell Fiona right away!*

She ran down the hall to the cluster of rooms that were being used for changing, but when she got to the one for Fiona, she was met outside the door by Philip. "Paige, isn't it? Fiona's friend. What can I help you with?"

"I need to talk to Fiona."

He shook his head. "Afraid that's not a good idea. She gets terribly nervous before a performance and needs to be by herself. Can I deliver a message instead?"

Paige fumed, but admitted he had a point. The last thing she should do was upset Fiona before her performance. Spotting a cameraman coming down the hall, inspiration struck. "Philip, do you know who that is?"

"Yes, he's part of the crew I hired to document Fiona's performance."

Her pulse ticked. "He works for you?" Philip nodded and Paige grinned. "That's perfect! Can I borrow him for, like, fifteen minutes?"

Philip agreed and introduced her to the cameraman, whom Paige led into the church. Scanning the crowd, she soon spotted Liam. *If I have my way, Liam Hart, you will never bother Fiona again!*

"Liam?" Paige stood behind him, speaking softly. "I need to talk to you, privately. I'm afraid I've got some terrible news."

His ruddy face hardened at her words. "Oh, don't tell me that Fiona's having second thoughts."

"No, nothing like that. Fiona's fine. Just, can we talk over here?" She led him to the quiet alcove, where the cameraman stood waiting. "Fiona's fine, Liam. It's you I'm worried about."

He stared blankly, appearing unconcerned.

"You see, Liam, we've had a camera crew here all day to document the concert. See, there he is right there." She waggled her fingers at the cameraman and he gave a curt nod in return.

"Yeah, so?" Liam's eyes darted around the alcove, not paying particular attention.

"So, remember when you were talking to your buddy, Russell, about your beloved cousin Alice, the one who was much too pretty to be a lesbian? And about, oh, destroying private property to drive her and her girlfriend off the land so they'd sell?"

Liam's eyes grew large as saucers and his face deepened to the shade of a fine claret wine. "That's...I don't know what you heard, but that's not what I said."

Her heart racing, Paige feigned calm. "Oh, I think we both know it is. And so does my cameraman." The man gave another nod, on cue. "Because he got it all on tape."

Paige was fairly certain Liam had stopped breathing, and decided to go in for the kill. "I see I have your full attention now. You know, that's not even the most interesting thing about you that I've heard lately. I had a little conversation with Harry the other day, and the figures he told me for ticket sales and the figures you reported as projected profit from this event aren't even close."

"Well, there's nothing wrong there. That's just my organizing fee that the charity's paying me."

She laughed triumphantly inside her head. It had been a hunch, but it seemed she'd been right. "You're right. There's nothing illegal about that, even if a few people on the committee may feel a little like they've been duped. But that's why people are going to be so impressed when you decide not to accept that fee, and instead give it all to Alice's charity."

"That's...I'm..."

Paige was starting to get concerned about Liam's unhealthy coloration, but she continued. "Or I could arrange a world premiere of your new film." *The film that doesn't really exist...* Would he call her bluff and demand to see it? She needed to make this convincing. "I know I'm new here, but you know what I've noticed? There are a lot of people in the village who loved Alice. Like *really* loved, not just trying to grab her land or make some money off her memory. You've been here a lot longer than me. In fact, I imagine you probably do business with a lot of these people. Like, a lot of them. How do you think they'd feel if they knew how you really felt?"

He fell silent, looking frightened. She wasn't surprised. He was the schoolyard bully who backed down when someone confronted him on his own level. And it seemed Paige's guess had hit a nerve. He needed his reputation more than Fiona's farm.

His eyes narrowed. "Why do you care? You didn't even know my cousin."

"True." She drew a steady breath, tamping down the anger she felt toward him and his kind. "But I know you, and people like you. As long as you're around, us *dykes* gotta stick together. Yes, that's on the film, too."

"So, how do I get this film?"

Her heart raced at the demand she should have seen coming, but thankfully, her mind was quick. *Play it cool.* "You don't. That belongs to me. And don't think you can try to take it, either. The copy is safe, and even if you got a hold of it, my man here knows everything you said, same as me. People might think I had an axe to grind, but no one's going to doubt his word."

Liam nodded sullenly, looking at the floor.

"Just so we understand each other, in order to keep this from public view: no organizing fee and no more sabotaging the Blake farm. Oh, and after the holidays, you're stepping away from any involvement in Alice's charity." She ticked them off on her fingers, one by one.

He nodded again, this time glaring at her.

"Pleasure working with you, Liam," she called as he stormed away. Paige turned to the cameraman. "Thank you for your help. We're all set, I think." The man responded in Polish, and Paige reflected that it was a good thing Liam was far enough away not to discover that her witness didn't speak a word of English.

EIGHTEEN

RETURNING in triumph to the sanctuary, Paige took a seat with the audience and spent the next two hours transported, enraptured by Fiona's voice. From the first note, Paige felt chills. It was the same angelic voice as in the Black Fleece, but so much more. *She's born to do this.* Unlike Paige, who preferred a smaller crowd, the energy of the audience brought Fiona to life, imbuing her performance with an ethereal quality that was lacking in a more humble venue. Fiona's voice was meant for multitudes.

In the last act, she stood on stage, literally looking like a host of the heavenly realm brought down to earth just for them. Her white, floor-length evening gown sparkled along every curve. *A really sexy angel*, Paige thought, and hoped she wouldn't be struck by lightning for thinking about an angel that way, but it was true. Fiona was an angel without the wings—*which would have been cheesy*, she thought, stifling a giggle at the image that formed in her mind. Also no halo. That might have been pushing it. It wasn't like Fiona went around *acting* like an angel all the time, for which Paige was just as pleased. And then the music played and she began to sing, and all Paige's silly jokes fled from her mind, replaced with pure awe and reverence at the enormity of Fiona's talent. To think when they'd met, she'd had no idea!

"Fee!" Paige called out when she reached Fiona's dressing room door backstage. This time, Philip let her in without a moment's hesitation. "You were amazing!" She threw her arms around her and squeezed so tightly that Fiona started to cough.

"Careful there," Philip said with a laugh. "You can't damage the star! And she's going to be, I guarantee it. A bigger star than ever before, if I have anything to do with it!"

Fiona rolled her eyes with a laugh. "He's been talking like that all day. And hovering over me like a mother hen, blocking the door so no one could bother me. He said you stopped by?"

"I did…" The whole sordid story of her encounters with Liam perched on the tip of her tongue, ready to spill. But she looked at Fiona, still dressed in her white gown and flushed from her triumphant comeback, and she couldn't tell her. "I just came by to wish you luck, but clearly you didn't need it." Fiona beamed and kissed her, and Paige knew she'd made the right choice. There was no need to let someone like Liam spoil Fiona's day.

They were among the last to leave the church, and the snow had been falling steadily all afternoon. The wind whipped along the narrow road up as they drove, and the conditions steadily worsened to a near whiteout. Though the drive was only a few miles long, at one point they had to pull off to the side of the road to wait out a particularly heavy squall.

"I just hope the guests all made it back safely to the Black Fleece," Paige said, her voice a nervous half-whisper as she stared into the storm. "And that we do, too."

"We'll be fine." Fiona's confidence provided relief. "And the guests would have traveled back an hour ago. I think we're seeing the worst of the snow just now. My concern is for the fences. With all the trouble they give me, I doubt they'll hold."

"I wouldn't worry." Paige smiled enigmatically, looking like a cross between the Mona Lisa and a cat that ate a canary. "In fact, I wouldn't be surprised if those fences hold a whole lot better from now on."

The front of the Black Fleece was dark when they finally arrived in the village. The pub was closed to prepare for the big dinner the following day. Even knowing the reason, Paige felt a chill run through her, the lack of light foreboding and strange. But once they went inside, the warmth returned. There was plenty of movement and laughter coming from upstairs, where

Paige knew that the guests were enjoying sandwiches and a fire in the sitting room.

They'd just stopped for a quick check on preparations, so they opted to stay downstairs. Fiona wasn't just the owner of the inn but the star of the evening, after all, and the guests upstairs were her fans. If they went up for even a minute, they might never get away. Instead, they sneaked into the kitchen. As they approached the door, Paige's sense of foreboding returned. It was quiet. Too quiet. Pushing open the door to find the once-bustling kitchen empty, Paige's stomach tightened.

"Where is everyone?"

Fiona took in the space with a frown. "I don't know. Maybe Maria sent the staff home early because of the storm."

Paige jumped as a moan broke the silence. Following the direction of the sound, her breath caught to discover Maria, slumped in a chair and doubled over.

"Maria!" Paige cried out. "Are you okay?"

Maria moaned, louder this time. "I think my water broke."

Paige's breathing sped up. "Why are you alone?

"We finished early and I sent everyone home before the snow got too bad. I was just heading out myself when it happened. I've tried Brandon, but he isn't picking up. And then the pain got so bad I had to sit."

Fiona knelt beside the chair and took Maria's hand. "Is an ambulance on its way?"

She shook her head. "I didn't even think of it."

Paige dug in her purse for her phone. "I'll dial 911."

Fiona cocked her head, giving Paige a funny look. "You mean 999?"

She slapped a hand to her forehead. "Yes! I knew that. I'm just a little freaked out."

She dialed and an operator answered, but when Paige requested an ambulance and gave her the address, the woman apologized profusely while explaining that it could take a long time to reach their part of the valley because of the storm. Paige held the phone away from her mouth and told Fiona the bad news.

"Give them the address of your cottage instead, then."

"Why?"

"Because she might have this baby before they get here, and if she does, it's probably best not to do it in the kitchen with thirty guests upstairs."

Paige felt sick. "Good point. But why my cottage?"

"You were planning to sleep with me tonight anyway." She it so matter-of-factly that Paige began to laugh.

"Oh I was, was I?" she teased. Fiona raised an eyebrow in response. "Okay, okay. I was." Paige gave the operator the address.

"Do you think you can walk?" Fiona asked, and Maria nodded.

They helped her up and into the car, and drove it ever so slowly up the hill. The street was icy and the tires fishtailed wildly, leaving a crooked path in the snow. The thought of an ambulance making a similar trek left Paige shaky.

"Paige, help her inside. I'm going to look for Brandon in the barn."

Her shakiness became more pronounced as they waited inside, Maria's low moans the only sound other than the shrieking of the wind. Finally Paige stood, pacing the room to maintain control. "How long does it take to check the barn?"

Maria struggled to sit up straight. "He might be out looking for a missing sheep." Worry etched Maria's brow, and Paige realized that giving voice to the frantic questions probably racing through her mind was only making things worse.

"I'm sure they'll be back any minute." She mustered all the confidence she possessed as she said it.

Finally, the cottage door opened, revealing Fiona and Brandon covered head to toe in snow, but safe. A relieved cry echoed through the room, and Paige wasn't sure if it had been her or Maria who made it.

Brandon rushed to Maria's side while Paige and Fiona stared awkwardly at the scene. Brandon tried to get a closer look, but Maria yelped and pushed his hands away.

"Oh, no! You're not putting those ice blocks anywhere near my private bits, Mister!"

Paige clamped her hand over her mouth, pent-up laughter caused tears to pool in the corners of her eyes.

"Let's go boil some water," Fiona suggested, her twitching mouth revealing her own struggle to keep a straight face.

"Right. For the baby." Paige made the declaration with more confidence than she felt, since she didn't know the first thing about childbirth. "They always do that in the movies."

Fiona looked blankly at her. "No, for tea." Her shoulders shook in silent mirth.

"I don't have any tea." Paige bowed her head sheepishly at Fiona's horrified expression. "I have coffee. I don't really like tea." Though the last part was mumbled, there was little hope Fiona hadn't caught it.

"But...but I make tea for you every morning!" It was difficult to tell if she was hurt by the revelation, or merely confused as to why someone would choke down something they didn't like on a daily basis without saying a word about it.

"I like it when you make it," Paige reassured her, then cringed as Maria let out a scream. "I think I'll go make coffee. Right now." She ran from the living room as quickly as she could.

As Paige filled the kettle and scooped the coffee into the French press on the counter, Fiona joined her.

"I think Maria needed some privacy," Fiona explained in a hushed tone. "Brandon's got it under control."

"Does he know how to deliver a baby?"

"Well, he delivers lambs all the time. How different can it be?" A grin cracked Fiona's face as Paige's eyes threatened to pop out of her head. "That was a joke! He's got the operator on the phone again, talking him through what to do until the ambulance arrives. They're twenty minutes away."

They stood in the kitchen, holding each other by the hand and sipping coffee (Fiona mostly containing her grimace) until finally, the bright lights of the ambulance came flashing up the hill. A harried Brandon poked his head through the kitchen door.

"Paige, she's calling for you."

"Me?" Paige gulped. *What does she want with me?*

The paramedics had loaded Maria onto a gurney and were preparing to wheel her outside when Paige came into the room. "Paige, come here." Paige approached and Maria grasped a fistful of fabric from her shirt and pulled her closer. Paige gulped. "I know you know how to cook. My girls will be back in the morning, but some of them are new. They need someone to keep an eye on everything and help them through." Maria grimaced as a new contraction began. "I've left a list of what needs to be done for Christmas dinner on the counter in kitchen at the Black Fleece. I'm leaving *you* in charge. Keep them on task, Paige. We *cannot* afford a mistake!" Paige wasn't certain what the penalty would be for turning her down, or God forbid screwing up the meal itself, but she suspected from the intensity of her stare that an ancient curse might be invoked. Eyes wide, Paige nodded.

Paige stared after Maria as she was taken to the ambulance, her palms sweating as if the cook had just left her in charge of nuclear launch codes. *Me? In charge?* She was about to cook the biggest dinner of her life, and it was all her own fault, too. If it hadn't been for her insistence on opening the inn and making a last-minute marketing push, they wouldn't be expecting over two hundred people for dinner at the Black Fleece in less than twenty-four hours. She'd done a whole lot more meddling than she'd intended since she'd arrived in Holme, and now all those chickens were coming home to roost. She just hoped she wouldn't be expected to fry them up in time for lunch.

IT WAS five o'clock in the morning when Paige and Fiona stumbled into the kitchen at the Black Fleece. Actually, Fiona, whose duties on the farm frequently required getting up before the sun, did more of a casual stroll. It was only Paige who tripped over her own feet. Thankfully, the storm had stopped and the snow gleamed white in the moonlight. It would have been a beautiful sight if Paige hadn't been focused on the fact that the moon was up instead of the sun.

Fiona switched on lights and Paige scanned the space quickly, spotting the note Maria had left for her, but not yet having gathered the courage to look at it.

"So, what do you eat in this country for Christmas, anyway?"

"What do we eat?" Fiona shrugged. "Same thing everyone eats, I guess. Turkey, stuffing, potatoes..."

Paige breathed a sigh of relief. The familiarity of the fare gave her confidence a much needed boost. "I can handle that, no problem. That's what we have for Thanksgiving."

Fiona scratched her head. "Thanksgiving's the one in November? Then what do you have for Christmas?"

"Chinese food." Paige chuckled, anticipating Fiona's confusion. "My mom liked the easiness of picking up take-out, and then Veronica's family was from Taiwan, so..."

"Not exactly the same thing as an English Christmas then."

"Not exactly. I mean, most people have turkey, just not us. But I cook a mean turkey in cider brine, and my mashed potatoes are smooth as—"

Fiona frowned. "Mashed? We usually roast them."

Paige nodded sharply, making a mental note. "Okay, I know how to do that. Now, for the candied yams—what?" She stopped as Fiona's eyebrows shot up to her hairline.

"What do you mean what?"

"You're looking at me funny."

Fiona's face scrunched. "I'm not exactly certain what a yam is. We might have had them when I was young, but I'm not certain. Maybe we call them something else?"

"It's an orange vegetable. They come in a can and you cook them with brown sugar and marshmallows on top."

Fiona's face filled with disgust. "Dear God, why?"

"Tradition I guess." Paige shrugged. "I take it you don't do those here, but that's fine. They're not really my favorite vegetable."

"We usually just have normal vegetables, maybe with a little bit of butter. Boiled carrots, roasted parsnip, some mashed swede—what?" She stopped as suddenly as Paige had before.

"I'm not certain what a swede is. Maybe we call them something else?"

"They're a big, roundish sort of a root that's purple and orange and waxy…"

"Oh, a turnip!" Paige clapped her hands as if she'd answered a question correctly on a gameshow.

"Yes!" Fiona clapped her hands, too. "I knew they had another name."

"And you mash those?" The shadow of doubt passed over Paige's face, but she chased it away with a bright smile. "Never mind, I'm sure I can figure it out."

Fiona drew a sharp breath. "Oh! Sprouts! It wouldn't do to forget those."

"Brussels sprouts? I love those!" Paige licked her lips as her expression grew dreamy. "I make them in a maple syrup reduction, sprinkled with chopped pecans...and you're doing it again." Paige wondered what quirk of British cuisine was about to be revealed to her this time.

"What? No I'm not."

"Yes you are. You're looking at me funny." She placed her hands on her hips. "How am I ruining the sprouts?" She said it so sternly that it was obvious she was joking.

"You put syrup on sprouts and marshmallows on the other things...the yams. You know they're vegetables, right?"

"You just don't understand, obviously." Paige shook her head in dismay. "Please tell me you use cranberry sauce for your turkey?"

"Of course."

"Well, you were so anti-sweet things, I was getting worried," Paige grumbled teasingly.

"And pigs in a blanket."

Paige blinked. "For what?"

This time Fiona shook her head, as if she couldn't believe it wasn't obvious. "The turkey. It's sort of a garnish, like the cranberry sauce." She wagged her finger as Paige made a gagging motion. "Don't look at me like that, it's good! Nice salty bacon and sausage to go with all that tasteless turkey…"

Paige's head was swimming with all the ways in which the dinner she'd thought she would be making wasn't at all what she'd expected. "So what does that leave?"

"Just dessert, I think. Which is usually Christmas pudding."

Paige sighed in relief. "Oh, I know exactly what that is because I helped Maria make it weeks ago! I guess the best part is we just have to reheat them."

"And set them on fire."

"You're making that up."

Fiona shook her head. "I'm really not. But we'll put one of the servers on it, if you'd rather."

Paige nodded gratefully. Setting things on fire should be left to the experts. "What about pie?"

"Of course!"

"Oh thank goodness!" As much as she adored Fiona, if this country didn't have pie, she was afraid she wouldn't be coming back. "I make a pumpkin pie that's just to *die* for."

Again, Fiona's eyebrows launched upward. "Why would you do that to a pumpkin? It's yet *another* vegetable you've added sugar to! What is it with Americans turning vegetables into puddings? The only proper pie for Christmas is mince pie."

"Mince, like mincemeat?" Paige stuck out her

tongue in revulsion. "It's okay to make a dessert from meat, but not from a perfectly good pumpkin? What do you have against pumpkins?"

"I don't think mince has real meat in it anymore. And I don't have anything against pumpkins, personally. I told you, I grew up in the Caribbean. My mother makes a fantastic pumpkin soup. I'll get the recipe from her next year and we can try the soup and the pie and figure out which one is better."

A warm glow spread through Paige's insides, radiating from her heart. "That sounds good. Especially the part about next year." Their eyes locked and she smiled shyly, wondering if Fiona had meant it seriously. The look in her eyes told her she had. They stood in silence for a moment, not needing words to understand that neither wanted to have to say goodbye.

Finally, Fiona spoke. "So, you still think you can handle the dinner?" She asked not as a challenge, but with real concern, and Paige knew that if she said she couldn't Fiona would find another way. "You don't have to, you know. It's my responsibility, and I'll find a way to manage."

"Don't be silly. Cooking a big holiday dinner? I *live* for this kind of thing!" Her shoulders squared and she lifted her chin. "But I think I've learned that our food is a lot like our countries. Exactly the same, but really different."

"Like our spelling."

"And driving," Paige said, shuddering.

She checked the time on the big kitchen clock. "Time to get started. The cooking staff will be arriving soon. You need to go turn on your star power to wow the guests." She grabbed Maria's list from the counter and read it through. It wasn't as frightening as she'd feared, and joking with Fiona like she'd done made her feel brave. Two hundred people for Christmas dinner? *Bring it on!* "Okay, Fee. Time to save Christmas!"

NINETEEN

EVERY MUSCLE and joint in Fiona's body protested as she and Paige began the ascent from the Black Fleece to the farmhouse. They walked in peaceful silence, enjoying the calm after a hectic day. The soft glow of hearths and tree lights shone from the windows of the village's weathered buildings that they passed, making squares of light in the snow. The scent of pine boughs, and cinnamon, and wood smoke perfumed the air. Flakes were falling once again, no longer a winter storm but the pleasant, swirling type that made it feel like Christmas had truly arrived.

In fact, Fiona realized with a sense of disbelief, Christmas was nearly over—and they hadn't yet had a chance to celebrate! The festival, the storm, and serving Christmas dinner—not to mention the arrival of a baby!—had all seemed a part of one extremely long, yet satisfying day.

With stars and moon obscured by the stormy sky, by the time they reached the top of the hill the only visible light was from the houses nestled in the valley below. From the vantage point of the farmhouse, the tiny hamlet of Holme looked like a Christmas village displayed in piles of cotton wool on top of someone's mantle. The farmhouse was dark as they approached, at odds with the cheeriness surrounding them. With a stab of regret, Fiona realized that in the effort to make sure all of the guests at the inn had a happy Christmas, her own preparations were sorely lacking. Though Paige's company was sufficient to make it a happy holiday, Fiona wished she'd thought to do something special to brighten up her drab home.

Her arms were weighed down with containers of food from the day's feast, packed up in the kitchen of the Black Fleece for them to eat together at home. As she approached the front door, it occurred to Fiona that she wouldn't be able to reach the knob.

"Paige, can you manage the door, do you think?" she asked, breaking the silence.

"Sure. Can you hand me your key?"

Fiona chuckled. "You should have noticed by now that I never lock the door. No one around here does."

"Daniel did," Paige pointed out, and Fiona laughed some more as she recalled the unusual circumstances of Paige's arrival in Holme.

"Good thing he did, too. Otherwise we might not have met."

Paige raised an eyebrow. "Seriously, Fee? I can see my cottage from your doorstep. How would we not have met?"

"Because I would never have got up the courage to talk to you," she confessed. "My boldness that first night was a singular occurrence."

"Good point. Me, too."

"I suppose at least neither of us will have to worry about the other straying when we're apart." She'd said it as a joke, but the reminder of that eventuality drained the smile from her lips. "Get the light, too, would you?" she directed, still juggling the bags and boxes of food as they stepped into the front hall.

At the snap of the switch, Fiona and Paige gasped collectively. The living room beside them was bathed in light, but not of the type that either of them had been expecting. The usual lonely lamp in the window had been replaced by a towering pine tree wrapped in sparkling white fairy lights, tinsel, and baubles.

"How did that get here?" Fiona breathed.

Paige laughed heartily. "I asked Brandon to bring it over yesterday morning, but we got so busy, I completely forgot!"

Fiona joined in the laughter. "You should have seen your face! You were at least as shocked by it as I was! It's beautiful, though. Thank you."

"It was mostly Brandon, really. Poor guy, I feel kind of bad. If I had realized he and Maria were going to have a baby later in the day, I wouldn't have asked him to do so much work!"

"Nobody was expecting that. She was still several weeks away from being due."

"How are they, have you heard?"

"Yes! I got a message not half an hour ago. Everyone is doing just fine. They had a baby girl, Grace." Fiona's voice shook with emotion as she shared the happy news.

"Oh, I'm so glad!"

Her throbbing biceps reminded her of the packages that still filled her arms. She'd been so caught up in admiring the tree that she'd nearly forgotten about them. Heading to the kitchen now, she set them down on the counter and turned to Paige. "Do you want to eat in the dining room?" Her question lacked enthusiasm. Though her stomach rumbled, the prospect of sitting down in the formal space left Fiona cold.

"Is it terrible if I say no?" Paige replied. "The tree is so beautiful, maybe we could eat in the living room?"

Her heart sang—she and Paige were so in tune. "That's exactly what I was thinking, too!"

"I'll fix our plates. You go figure out a place for us to sit."

Somewhere in the living room, Fiona knew that there was a large blanket that would make the perfect place to set up a picnic on the floor. She scoured the room, sighing when she spotted the pile of plaid wool.

"Oh, Maxie. Did you have to choose that spot for your nap instead of the bed?"

The dog opened one eye cautiously, as if contemplating whether Fiona deserved her cooperation after leaving her home alone for two days. But then she stood and moved from the blanket. Fiona spread it out on the floor beside the couch, and Maxine padded back over when she'd finished, reclaiming a spot on the far corner.

After lighting a fire in the fireplace, Fiona settled in, too, gazing at the Christmas tree and reflecting on the day and its improbable success. While Paige had kept things running behind the scenes, she'd had a chance to greet all of the customers as they arrived. The guests had been comprised of both neighbors and fans, of people who had traveled a great distance just to hear her voice, and others who lived and worked beside her every day and had walked just a few steps to show their support. To make her welcome.

After performing in public Christmas Eve, Fiona once again found her life split between a career in music and her duties on the farm. Philip was already gearing up, considering her reemergence onto the stage to be just the first step in her comeback tour. After spending much of the past year avoiding them both, she was surprised to realize that she loved both parts of her life, the quiet of the country and the thrill of the spotlight, as much as she held deep reservations about each.

Dread crept through her belly at the prospect of having to choose. *Which could make me happier?* She couldn't have both. She'd tried that approach before when Alice was alive, and look where that had led. Complete ruin. She stared at the flickering fire on the hearth and felt a kinship with the burning logs. In the end, she'd failed Alice at her moment of greatest need, lost the joy she'd found in her music, and was left with nothing but ashes.

Her thoughts had traveled this path before, many times, falling deeper into the darkness. But this time she found her heart lifted back into light. This year, Christmas had been the perfect blending of home and public lives, of sitting in harmony around one table. Having both, she felt complete, and in her heart she knew that Paige had made all the difference.

She'd struggled to see how these aspects of her life could coexist in part because Alice hadn't been able to see it. With roots as deep as hers, she'd found it impossible to accept that Fiona could both travel the world and remain connected to home. So she'd pulled her subtly closer to home at every turn, and Fiona had responded in turn by pulling away. She'd done it subtly, too, but the effects had been real. Why else had she resisted proposing to Alice until it was too late?

"You look lost in thought," Paige said as she set down their dinner plates and snuggled beside Fiona on the blanket. "Are you okay?"

Fiona smiled reassuringly. "Just pensive." Though her future was far from clear, her spirit felt at peace in a way it hadn't in a long time. Maybe ever.

When they'd finished eating, Fiona cleared their plates. Moments later, she emerged from the kitchen balancing a plate of brightly flaming Christmas pudding. Paige clapped in delight.

"A spoon for you, and a spoon for me," Fiona said, placing the plate between them. "When you were helping Maria with the Christmas pudding, did she tell you how it's a tradition for everyone to take a turn stirring and make a wish?"

Paige's eyes sparkled, sending a ripple of happiness through Fiona's heart. "Yes, she did! She even made sure I took my turn."

"What did you wish for?"

"Nothing." Paige frowned. "I couldn't think of anything at the time, so I saved it for later. Do you think it works that way?"

Fiona pondered this as if it were a serious question. "I don't pretend to be an expert on the statute of limitations for Christmas magic, but I think you could make a case for it. You probably wouldn't get a punishment for trying, anyway."

Paige nodded, satisfied. "Then I wish I could stay, just a little bit longer." Just in case she, too, had an unclaimed wish somewhere on her cosmic balance sheet, Fiona closed her eyes and wished the same.

With a laugh, the women dug their spoons into the dense, dark pudding, each lifting a steaming bite to their lips. As she pulled the spoon into her mouth, Paige jumped at the sound of an incoming message on her phone.

"Probably from my family, wishing me a merry Christmas."

As she pulled out her phone, Fiona's phone began to buzz, too, and her brother's face popped up on her screen.

"Daniel! Happy Christmas!" She spoke in that extra loud voice reserved for phone calls with people who can hear you just fine but are an especially long distance away.

"Hi, Fee! Happy Christmas! How are things at the farm?"

"Oh, well, you know…" Fiona's brow furrowed as Paige jabbed her in the ribs. "I think I'm finally figuring it out, Daniel. You were right all along."

"As I knew I would be, darling. You just needed a push."

"Oh, we got some snow!"

"Snow for Christmas! What good luck! Has it been very cold?"

"Fee?" Paige whispered, nudging her again. "Fee! Look at this!"

Fiona's expression reflected the full exasperation of an Englishwoman interrupted while discussing the weather. "What?" she mouthed, covering the phone with one hand. Paige shoved her phone in Fiona's face. A picture filled the screen, of Daniel standing in a room with red velvet drapes. A woman stood beside him in a white dress, and a somewhat pudgy man in an Elvis costume stood between them. Fiona blinked several times, her head spinning.

"It's your brother and my best friend!" Paige's voice grew louder. "At the Velvet Elvis!"

"The what?" Fiona spoke in a full volume now, though she still covered the phone.

"It's a wedding chapel in Reno!"

Fiona uncovered the phone. "Daniel," she began with exceeding calm, "Where are you right now?"

"America, Fee. I explained in my note, remember?"

"Daniel. Paige has just shown me a photograph of you and her best friend at a wedding chapel. Is this a little Christmas joke?"

"What's Paige doing there?" Daniel deflected. *"Isn't it rather late?"*

"Daniel," Fiona admonished, having had just about enough of joking, "is there something you aren't telling me?"

"It's real. Oh my God, it's real!" Paige gesticulated wildly. "Brittany just sent a dozen more pictures! Hold on, I'm going to call her now."

Several more pictures and a brief chat with Elvis confirmed the story. Daniel and Brittany had tied the knot.

Holy shit. "My brother is an idiot." Fiona massaged her temples gently. "Your best friend, too, no offense."

Paige nodded. "None taken. I think I should call my

mother and break the news that *I'm* the responsible one, now."

Fiona's thoughts whirled. "How's Daniel going to finish school? Where will he work?"

"Where will they live?"

"America apparently. I understand his new wife—oh my God, my brother has a wife—I guess she owns a house?"

"Yeah. *My* house. At least, I lived there, too." Paige frowned. "Where am I going to live?" Fiona's eyes brightened with the beginnings of an idea, but Paige cut her short. "And don't say here. We're the responsible ones, remember? Besides, I'm not ready to move a million miles from home."

Fiona slumped. "It was just a thought."

Snuggling against Fiona's shoulder, Paige rested her head. "And one I appreciate. But it's too soon, and no matter how much I know you want me to stay, I'm sticking with what I know is right from now on. I guess I could stay with my parents. Maybe go to LA for a few weeks. I have a film score to deliver to Mike. I could go back to some of my old gigs, I guess. Maybe teach music lessons."

"Couldn't you do that here, though?"

"Not legally. And I can only live on savings for so long. Which, incidentally, isn't much longer, although you've been feeding me so many nights, I've hardly spent any money while I've been here."

"I could keep doing that. It's the least I could do, to repay all the work you've done for me, if nothing else." Fiona closed her eyes and pulled Paige closer against her. "Tell me the truth, Paige. If you could, would you stay?"

"I would love to stay longer, Fee. Just not forever."

"Is that a never forever, or just a not now, or…"

Paige laughed softly. "Just not now. We both have huge changes ahead and I don't think either one of us knows enough of what's in store to jump in too deep."

Fiona nodded, knowing Paige was right. "Unlike Daniel and Brittany."

Paige groaned. "I still can't believe it." She sat up straight. "But they did it, and now my best friend is your sister-in-law. You know what this calls for? Champagne! I think I saw some in your fridge." She jumped up, taking the untouched plate of Christmas pudding with her.

Still reeling from her brother's announcement, Fiona leaned her head back against the sofa and closed her eyes. With a whimper, Maxine trotted across the blanket and curled herself into a ball beside her. Returning with glasses and the champagne bottle, Paige settled back into her spot with Maxine between them. At the loud popping of the cork, Maxine buried her nose under Paige's thigh.

Fiona looked down at the dog and shook her head. "Whatever the future might hold, we both need to take into consideration just how much my dog likes you."

"She likes everyone!" Paige handed Fiona one of the filled flutes.

Fiona shook her head as she took the glass. "She really doesn't. Although the only one she hates is Dolly."

Paige laughed. "Poor Dolly. Although, I did see them sniffing at each other a few mornings ago in an almost friendly way. I think they're becoming friends."

Fiona rolled her eyes, thinking of Daniel. "Next thing you know, *they'll* elope."

"Everyone's doing it." Paige winked. "I guess there's hope for us, yet."

Fiona turned her head and looked at Paige, her heart swelling just from the sight. "You know what? We can think about this another time. It's Christmas. Happy Christmas, Paige."

Clinking glasses chimed like a tiny bell.

"Merry Christmas, Fee." The look in Paige's eyes filled Fiona with hope and peace. "It's the perfect Christmas, you know," Paige whispered. "There's snow falling outside, but not too much. Just some big, gentle flakes."

"Starting with the weather. Well done. We'll make you into an Englishwoman yet."

"There's a newborn baby."

Fiona lifted her glass again. "To Maria, Brandon, and little Grace!"

"We have a barn full of animals, and an angel singing…"

"There weren't any angels. You're starting to hallucinate," Fiona replied dryly. "Do we need to go to Dr. Ross again?"

"I disagree. I heard an angel yesterday. Even saw her in the flesh."

Fiona pressed her lips together to keep from grinning. "Is that right?" she pressed. "You're sure you didn't see a shepherd instead?"

"Well, as it happens, she's both. But when I saw her, she was an angel. She was wearing this very slinky white dress, which gave me the *most* inappropriate thoughts. If I were Catholic, I'd probably have to go to confession."

Fiona nuzzled her lips just below Paige's earlobe. "If you asked really nicely, you might get the vicar to hear your confession."

Paige doubled over in silent laughter. "Oh, God. No!" She looked at Fiona and continued to laugh, until the laughter faded and they sat quietly gazing into each other's eyes. Paige's lips twitched into a self-conscious smile. Placing one hand behind Fiona's head, she pulled her closer until their lips met in a kiss. "You know what, it would take too long to list them all anyway. I think I'll just take my chances."

Fiona leaned in to return the kiss. At the taste of Paige's lips, desire coursed through her like a drug. She felt Paige's breath hitch and body shift closer, but as Fiona moved her leg to meet her halfway, she hit an immovable force. *Maxine*. One hand holding Paige's head so that her lips were in just the right place, she used the other to give the dog a few pointed nudges, but it was no use. Instead of moving, Maxine rolled onto her back and exposed her pink belly.

Fiona groaned in defeat. "I think we'll need to take this somewhere else."

"We will," Paige replied, stretching languidly in place. "But not yet. We have a Christmas tree to enjoy and the fire's still burning." She traced her finger in a winding path along Fiona's jaw, sending shivers to her core. "So just sit here and kiss me again. There's no rush."

Though their position was awkward and the canine between them insisted on interrupting on occasion with a thump of her tail or a nudge of her cold nose, Fiona couldn't remember ever experiencing a better kiss. The feel of Paige's lips against hers was thrilling. The exhilaration she felt as she explored the shape of Paige's body through the fabric of her blouse left Fiona breathless and desperate for more. But it went beyond that. It was a kiss that felt like home, that assured her that wherever life might take them, whatever far flung corners of the globe, she would only need the touch of those lips to be exactly where she belonged.

Paige had been right. It was the perfect Christmas. There was snow gently falling, a barn full of animals, a newborn baby, and angels singing. And between Paige's efforts and her own, there had been room for everyone this year at the inn. With a miracle like that, Fiona believed, whatever it might hold for them, the future would sort itself out just fine.

TWENTY

ONE YEAR Later

There was less than a week to go until Christmas as Paige looked out the kitchen window and across the harbor, the rays of summer sun increasing in intensity as they passed through the glass panes. Their short-term rental was situated in Kirribilli, a well-off suburb of Sydney. The houses were packed in tightly on small lots, but there still managed to be an abundance of leafy green trees, a reminder that the seasons were reversed from her usual hemisphere.

Paige chuckled as she recognized the tune she'd been humming: "I saw three ships come sailing in." It was a more appropriate Christmas carol than most for the location. Visible across the harbor was Sydney itself, where the white-sailed shape of the Opera House looked like the aforementioned ships. There would be no dreaming of white Christmases this year, or walking in winter wonderlands. Not that she was complaining. She liked Australia.

They'd arrived Down Under in the beginning of December and would stay until just after Fiona's performance at the New Year's Eve Gala. It was the longest they'd been together in one place in months, and Paige had almost started to think of their rented two-story house near the wharf as home. *Home* was a concept that had been mostly lacking in her life this year. Since leaving Fiona's farmhouse and heading back to the states, she hadn't really had a place to call home. After Mike's first film had found unexpected success on the film festival circuit, she'd spent some time in Los Angeles, working with him on a few other projects he'd had in the pipeline. Hollywood, with its thriving vintage club scene, was a great place for a jazz pianist, and she picked up gigs in fun, out-of-the-way places whenever she had the chance.

In between those jobs, she'd moved from place to place wherever she pleased. She spent those weeks composing music. The cottage swap had worked out so well that she'd signed up with a pet-sitting service that found her free places to stay in exchange for caring for pets while their owners were out of town. It was an ideal solution. Paige hadn't had much experience with dogs before going to Yorkshire, and she'd developed a fondness for Maxine. Being around other dogs helped ease the ache of separation.

When it came to Fiona, though, no substitute

would ever do. After leaving Holme at the end of January, she'd saved up to return for a visit at the beginning of June. Those four months in between had been the hardest of her life, especially with Fiona preparing for her world tour and not always available to answer her calls. When Fiona had embarked on her North American tour in September, they'd been able to spend time together every few weeks. Whenever they found themselves together, wherever they were, that was when Paige felt like she'd finally come home.

Part of her still questioned her decision not to stay in Holme from the very start, but she'd needed the time to sort out her feelings. She'd fallen into terrible habits in her years with Veronica, and made a lot of mistakes. She wanted to avoid repeating them. For her relationship with Fiona to succeed, she needed to know what she really valued and wanted out of life. But as another year drew to a close, more and more she found that answer was simple: what she wanted was Fiona. Where she lived or how she made her living paled in importance to being together.

Paige was sitting at the kitchen table, thumbing through the pages of a novel, when Fiona came in, her arms weighed down by a giant frozen turkey. She stumbled comically as Paige jumped up and rushed to relieve her of the burden.

They laughed as the two of them maneuvered the monster to the refrigerator. "Why did you get such a big turkey? It's only you and me, our parents, and Danny and Brit."

She felt a thrill of excitement as she listed off the names of their impending holiday guests. Fiona had convinced Philip to get travel expenses for every family member included in her contract, and they'd wanted her so badly that they'd signed without so much as blinking at the added cost. Paige still couldn't believe both their families would be gathered in one place for Christmas and New Year's Eve. She got butterflies just thinking about meeting Fiona's mom and dad for the first time. And based on a hunch, she planned to watch Brittany extra closely for any tell-tale hints of a baby bump.

It still felt strange to Paige to think of Fiona's hugely successful professional life. As far as she was concerned, Fiona was her most natural, truest self when she was walking along the long stone walls of her Yorkshire farm, checking for broken fences. Not that she needed to look too hard for those anymore. There hadn't been a single one in a year. For months, Fiona had tried to puzzle it out, but Paige just called it their Christmas miracle, and never breathed a word of what had happened. She chose to think that Alice would see it as a kindness to her that Fiona would never have to know about the Hart family's darker side.

The door on the refrigerator refused to close, and Paige rearranged some items and tried again. She gave it a good slam and it finally shut. "Let's hope the beast doesn't try to escape!"

"I'm so sorry, Paige. It was the only size they had. Do you think it will work?"

Paige dismissed the concern with a wave of her hand. "Of course. After last Christmas, it'll be nice to only be cooking *one* turkey, no matter how big. We'll just have a lot of leftovers. I hope they have cream of mushroom soup in this country, because my mom's from Minnesota and I'm about to introduce you to the culinary marvel that is *turkey hotdish*!"

Fiona blanched. "Dare I ask what it is?"

Paige flashed a particularly evil grin. "That's the beauty of it. It's anything you want it to be." Though Paige was a good cook, she'd taken a particularly perverse pleasure over the past year in introducing Fiona to some of the unique oddities of American cuisine.

"I had a letter from Brandon and Maria, along with a Christmas card." Fiona held up the card.

Paige cooed over the photo of little Gracie, nearly a year old now, and wearing an elf costume while seated on Dolly's back. To her astonishment, she saw that Maxine sat right beside her. "Well, look at that! Those two really do get a long now!"

Fiona chuckled. "Ever since Brandon and Maria took in Maxine while I've been away, she and Dolly have teamed up to keep Gracie out of trouble."

"It takes *both* of them to keep this little cherub in

line? Poor Maria! Are you really sure Dolly and Maxine are running the show, or is it the other way around?"

"Look at that child's face, and I think you'll have your answer."

"Poor Maxine and Dolly!" The picture made Paige feel unaccountably homesick as she thought of all the people back in Holme. She needed the most un-Yorkshire thing possible to distract her. "Do you want to go out to the pool?"

Taking advantage of the sun-filled summer day, they put on bathing suits, and Paige slid open the door that led to their secluded backyard with its flagstone patio and pool. The weather was sublime, with a pleasant sea breeze.

"I could get used to this," Fiona remarked as she followed a few steps behind.

Paige closed her eyes and tilted her face to the sun. "Me, too. I love the warm weather."

"Sure. That, too." Glancing back, Paige caught Fiona's eyes snaking along the length of her bikini-clad body. She licked her lips and pinched Paige's elastic waistband between two fingers, giving it a stretch.

"Later," she chided, swatting her hand away playfully. "First, I need to get some sun."

Fiona shrugged, looking defeated. "You'd tan better without the suit, is all I'm suggesting." Paige shot her a disbelieving look. "What? That's just a fact."

"Sure it is." The pool water was blue and inviting,

and Paige dipped her toes in to test it out. She pulled them out as fast as she could. "Brr! Still too cold."

The house was well furnished inside and out, and that included a two-piece sectional made of wicker that filled the patio, complete with a fancy fire pit. Paige had made the mistake of mentioning her intention to use it to make s'mores during their stay, which had earned her a lengthy lecture from Fiona about the American obsession with marshmallows. Then had come the crushing blow that Australia didn't have graham crackers.

Paige laughed silently. Little did Fiona know that Daniel was bringing three types of marshmallows— jumbo, mini, and rainbow— and a box of graham crackers in his suitcase when they arrived tomorrow. There would be a can of yams, as well. Brittany had made him a convert to the gooey potato dish, and candied yams were a delicacy Fiona had yet to try. Paige wondered if she could find the ingredients for green bean casserole, too, or if that many American dishes in one meal would break her girlfriend's spirit.

They reclined together on the sectional with their heads touching and their bodies extending away from each other at a ninety-degree angle along the thick outdoor cushions.

Fiona sighed happily. "You're right about the weather. It *is* nice here."

Paige uttered a quiet moan of approval. "As much

as I loved last Christmas in Yorkshire, I don't mind the lack of snow here."

"You did love it though?"

"Yorkshire? Of course. We've been a lot of places together this year, but there's no place like Holme." She chuckled at her terrible pun. Soon she realized it was very quiet. She knew the joke had been dumb, but it was unlike Fiona not to laugh even a little.

She opened her eyes and found Fiona propped up on her elbows, staring down at her. The odd juxtaposition of their faces threw off her perspective and made Paige feel dizzy. "What is it?"

"I really like the new color." She twisted the end of Paige's sapphire blue braid around her finger. "It suits you."

"So you told me yesterday when I had it done. But thank you again." Paige flushed at the compliment. "It was time for a change."

"Funny, that's what I've been thinking, too."

"You're *dyeing* your hair? Philip will kill you, you know."

"No, not my hair." Fiona's expression grew serious. "It's just, I've been thinking about this, and the tour's ending in a few months. After that, I'd really like to spend some time at home."

Paige smiled, relieved. With how Fiona had been looking, she'd expected something bad. "You want me to come visit?"

Fiona swallowed so loudly that Paige could hear her throat contract. "I want you to come live with me."

Happiness made her heart leap. Paige laughed and pulled Fiona's head towards hers, their mouths at an odd angle, but she really didn't care. After indulging in several passion-filled kisses, Fiona pulled away and sat up. "So, you'd consider that? You don't need more time to think about it?"

Paige sat up, too, cradling her body between Fiona's warm skin and the soft cushion behind her. Fiona took hold of her hand along the back of the couch and caressed her knuckles with her thumb. "I can't think of any place else I'd rather be than at the farm in Holme with you."

Fiona smiled, her eyes darting nervously. "In that case, there's just one other thing." Lightning fast, Fiona held Paige's hand in both of hers, and Paige's heart raced as she felt something warm and hard slide down the length of her left ring finger, encircling it. It felt solid, substantial, like the future that she and Fiona would share.

She snatched her hand away to see what had been placed there: a sparkling sapphire with tiny diamonds in a platinum art deco setting. She brought it up toward her face for a closer look and caught sight of it beside one of her braids. *It's exactly the same color as my hair!* Her pulse ticked so loudly in her ears that she almost missed the question, though she already knew the words. "Will you marry me?" She could see Fiona's pulse throbbing in her neck as she waited for the answer.

Paige's whole body trembled as she let herself fall into Fiona's embrace. "Yes! Of course, yes! I've never wanted anything so much."

Fiona pressed her lips to Paige's, then nibbled along her earlobe and jaw. Paige's hands clung to Fiona's neck, dizzy from so much stimulation. She stared at the blue stone on her finger in awe. It was unique and beautiful, just like the woman who'd given it to her. "Fiona? Where did you get this? It looks like an antique."

"It was my grandmother's." Fiona's lips traveled along her bare chest as she answered, making her shiver in delight.

"The one from the safe deposit box?" Butterflies swarmed her tummy. Fiona had told her the story of that ring before, a story of doubt and loss that today felt redeemed. Her brow wrinkled thoughtfully. "When did you have a chance to get it? You haven't been in London in months."

Fiona looked up from her vantage point on Paige's chest. "I went the day I took you to the airport in January. Even then, I knew it was always meant for you."

She twisted her hand in the sunlight, making the stone sparkle, and felt her heart swell with the knowledge of how much she loved Fiona, and how perfect the ring was, like it was made for her.

Wait... "Fee? Where were you keeping this?"

"Since January?" Fiona's fingers fiddled with the front clasp of her bikini top, pushing the fabric aside, producing sweet torture as thumbs brushed across nipples. A lightning bolt shot through her center at each caress.

"No," she gasped. "Just now." She forced herself to pull back just enough to scan Fiona's exposed, tan flesh and the itty-bitty bathing suit that pretended to cover it. "You don't exactly have pockets."

Fiona grinned. "Do you really want to know, or should I just..." She dipped her head and the rest of the words grew muffled as her tongue circles Paige's breast, sucking the hardened tip gently into her mouth.

Tears of pleasure stung Paige's eyes. "Never mind. I don't really need to know."

She shifted backward on the cushions, savoring Fiona's weight on top of her, her hands sliding along her skin, cupping her breasts, fumbling with the swimsuit ties. Fiona's mouth meandered between each of her breasts, finally settling in the valley between them, firm fingers massaging the sensitive mounds on either side.

Lost in the moment, she grasped Fiona's head, burying her fingers in her dark locks. The glint of the sun from the sapphire set in antique platinum held her gaze. She'd thought last Christmas in Fiona's farmhouse had been the perfect Christmas, but this one already had it beat. Last year she'd made a single wish, but this year all of her wishes had come true.

As Fiona's tongue continued down her abdomen, leaving a trail of goosebumps along her bare flesh, she stopped thinking altogether. There would be time for that later. In this perfect moment, she was content to let the love and desire they shared wash over her like the waves that lapped against the wharf in the distance. They'd finally both come home to where they belonged.

A MESSAGE FROM MIRANDA

Dear Reader,

Holme for the Holidays is the story of everything coming together just right to create the storybook Christmas. I was so fortunate to have had a chance to visit the real village of Holme in West Yorkshire while working on the book, and even had Sunday roast in the pub that inspired the Black Fleece Inn. For photos of the village that I took on my trip, please visit the blog on my website. And while, you're there, sign up for my email list!

Oh, in case you were wondering, some (but thankfully not all) of Paige's unfortunate travel mishaps are based on a true story… Also, that miniature coffee cup is totally real.

As always, reviews are the lifeblood of any author, so if you enjoyed the book and wouldn't mind going online and leaving a review, I would be forever grateful. And please accept my heartfelt thanks for the support you show in reading my work and recommending it to others.

Best Wishes,
Miranda

Printed in Great Britain
by Amazon